CANDLELIGHT REGENCY SPECIAL

CANDLELIGHT REGENCIES

LOVE
in
DISGUISE

Nina Pykare

A Candlelight Regency Special

Published by
Dell Publishing Co., Inc.
1 Dag Hammarskjold Plaza
New York, New York 10017

Dell ® TM 681510, Dell Publishing Co., Inc.

ISBN: 0-440-15229-1

Printed in the United States of America

First printing—February 1980

For lovers
in
every time
and
every place

LOVE
in
DISGUISE

Chapter One

The late August sun was stifling that day in London and anyone with a shred of sense had retired from the dust and heat of the city's sizzling pavements. Even the hardiest shrubs had withered and flies and wasps victimized those courageous few of the *ton* who had sought their courtyards for relief.

Most of the quality were far removed from the sultry, grimy city, enjoying themselves at their country seats. Or someone else's. Even those brave few who had elected—or had been forced—to spend the summer in the city were not about to venture forth into the glaring heat of the noonday sun.

And so no one, except perhaps a curious servant shielded by a curtain in an upstairs window, observed the dusty hackney coach draw up to the door of the fashionable house on St. James's Square. The servant did well to be curious, for the house had been empty these two months—since the death of the old Marquis of Cavendish, a crotchety old man, so reports had said. And eccentric. Queer in the upper story, in fact.

For the old man, having managed to outlive all his male relatives, had declared sworn hatred on his high-flown neighbors—for what cause none of them could say—and had left the house and an inheritance more than sufficient to maintain it to some bit of muslin. An actress from Bath, the whisperers said. Redhaired—and young.

The neighborhood looked forward to an interesting autumn if the story were true. For the house to the right of that before which the hackney had halted was the town residence of William, Earl of Morgane, a dark haughty man, whose right cheek carried a scar. Caused, so the gossipers said, by a duel in Germany in his youth. Only eighteen at the time, they said, and he had killed his man.

The driver of the hackney descended and began to unload several trunks and valises. The door of the carriage opened and a man climbed out, a huge man whose bald head reflected the sun. He turned to help a woman half his size, whose muslin dress and plain honest bonnet indicated her membership in the servant class.

The two stood in silent awe, surveying the house before them. It was obviously much grander than they had expected.

Suddenly from the interior of the carriage came a voice, sweet but strong. "Come, come, you two. Don't stand there gawking all day. Help me out so I can get a good look at this palace."

Both the man and the woman turned and in a moment the owner of the voice stood on the pavement. The sun could add no glory to the burnished copper of the curls that escaped her poke bonnet and the sprigged muslin gown that clung to her form revealed a figure that many a gentleman at Bath had pronounced excellent.

She surveyed the house through half-shut eyes—green eyes that warned of a fiery temper to match that hair. In silence the servants waited as their young mistress let her gaze travel from mahogany door to iron balconies to the terraced veranda roof. There was a moment's deep silence and then a piercing whistle split the afternoon's peace.

"Miss Fancy!" exclaimed the woman in alarm. But Miss Fancy only smiled. And then a howling, like that of a monster in pain, issued from the interior of the hackney.

The young woman turned to the man. "I forgot about Hercules, Henry. Do untie the poor thing. He must be stifling."

Henry nodded and entered the coach, emerging moments later with a gigantic English sheep dog who instantly put both paws on the young woman's shoulders, an action that would have laid any well-bred young lady out on the pavement in spasms. But the figure that had been pronounced excellent also hid strong muscles, and the young woman had obviously met such assaults before. She kept her feet.

"I love you, too, Hercules," she laughed, as the dog's great tongue just missed her ear. "Now get down and behave yourself."

Obediently the animal returned his front feet to the ground. For a few moments he surveyed the house and then, as though deciding against residence there, began to move toward the building on the right.

The man servant was large and strong, but it was all he could do to keep from being dragged along to the door of the Earl of Morgane.

"Hercules, no!" The sweet voice rang out. The dog stopped so quickly that the servant, huge as he was, was in danger of sitting down very swiftly.

The young woman laughed, a clear merry peal that had earned her the regard of many a Bath theatergoer. "Here, Henry, I'll take Hercules and you pay the driver. Then we'll see what my crotchety old cousin dumped on us."

The hackney driver, who had been watching the proceedings with the wooden face of a man long inured to peculiar happenings, could not forbear the slightest of grimaces. A house on St. James's Square! Sure, a queer old relative could dump the likes of such a house on him any day of the year!

Pocketing his money, the driver rattled off down the pavement. Life on St. James's Square would be

14

considerably livelier, he figured. With that redhead around things were bound to go topsy-turvy.

The girl, searching in her reticule, produced a key and handed it to the man. "Here, Henry. This should get us in."

"It's a terrible big place, Miss Fancy. Why, we'll be rattling around in there like a couple of bosky swells in an empty pit."

"Nonsense, Ethel," said the young woman. "My cousin, Cavendish, God rest his soul, meant for me to have this house and all its furnishings and enough blunt to keep it going. And I intend to do just that. Think how much room we shall have for clothes and things."

Ethel surveyed the rest of the Square and shook her head. Her plain face wrinkled into a frown. "This ain't no neighborhood for the likes of us, Miss Fancy. This is a place where great folks live."

The redhead sent forth another peal of laughter. "Never mind, Ethel. I intend to be great folks one of these days. I'll make it at Covent Garden, you'll see. Then I'll be as great as anyone."

Ethel shook her head but kept silent. There was no point in arguing with Miss Fancy when she had her mind set. No human being alive could be stubborner, as Ethel well knew.

During this conversation Henry had carried several valises to the door and succeeded in opening it. "Come, Miss Fancy. I'll bring the rest of the boxes."

*　*　*

And thus it was that Fancy Harper, late of the Bath Theatre and soon of Covent Garden, took up residence among the elite of St. James's Square.

The news was all over the neighborhood by dinner time, relayed by that most efficient mode of communication—servants. By the time the first course had been carried to the grand tables by the richly liveried footmen everyone on St. James's Square knew that *that* actress had arrived. Many of the gentlemen found themselves looking forward to the sight of their neighbor. Though the reports disagreed on particulars, they were in full accord on one matter—Fancy Harper was a stunner, a real beauty.

The ladies, of course, received this intelligence with something less than joy, speculating among themselves as ladies, particularly plain ones, are wont to do, concerning what it was about such creatures that could make their menfolk behave in such moon-calf fashion.

The servants could not believe that two menials were going to be able to manage a house that size. And those of them with friends or relatives looking out for a place began to lay plans for gaining the ear of the baldheaded giant. The little woman, judged by most to be his wife, was deemed to be powerless in such matters. The giant was the one to approach.

And so, life was considerably enlivened for the summer residents of St. James's Square, most of

16

whom were that evening engaged in considering what that redhead was likely to do next.

Certainly none of them could have imagined the scene that was at that moment taking place in the dining room of the great house. Miss Fancy Harper, her poke bonnet now removed and her copper curls swinging free, was seated at the huge table. Before her sat a plate of the finest silver, on whose shining surface lay a single piece of bread and butter, a slice of ham, and an apple.

"We got to have a cook, Miss Fancy," Ethel was complaining. "I can't manage this great house and all. It's too much for any mortal woman."

Fancy smiled. "Don't get yourself in a pet, Ethel. We'll have a cook—one of those Frenchmen—chefs, they call them. And maids. And—and—" She looked at Henry in dismay. "I really don't know *what* we need. Henry, can you find out?"

Henry nodded. "Yes, Miss Fancy, but it's going to take an awful lot of blunt."

"That doesn't signify," replied Fancy with a smile that had broken many a male heart in Bath. "We have money now. Cousin Cavendish saw to that." She laughed merrily. "The old gentleman did us up fine, he did. Too bad he couldn't leave me the title, too."

She took a bite of bread and butter and chewed thoughtfully. "But I guess it's better this way. It must be terrible stuffy to be one of the *ton*. Too stuffy for me."

She looked at the others with mischief in her

eyes. "Now if you two are going to insist on all this servant business, making me eat in this great room like some kind of high-in-the-instep lady, you'd better go get your own food. Because there's a multitude of things to be done in this place. And we're the only ones to do them. I want it all in order before Covent Garden opens the eighteenth of next month."

"Don't you be worrying your head none, Miss Fancy," replied Henry. "We'll have the place running smooth by then."

And Ethel, though she sighed heavily, nodded in agreement.

For several weeks the aristocracy on St. James's Square saw little of Miss Fancy Harper. True, there was a great deal of coming and going, trades-people and those vying for places in the actress's quickly growing establishment.

Henry presided over all the hustle and bustle in majestic calm. And before September was much along, he had hired the necessary additional servants, including a French chef with an unpronounceable name upon whose culinary efforts Ethel looked with a jaundiced eye, and a coachman and grooms to go with the several elegant carriages in the coach house. He had even, in the company of those worthies whose advice he found incomparable, taken a trip to Tattersalls and brought home the necessary horses.

And so, on an evening toward mid-September,

Miss Fancy Harper rose from the dinner table in her well-run establishment with a satisfied sigh. "That chef surely knows how to put together food," she remarked to the waiting Henry and the footmen who seemed to her to be lining the walls.

She pushed back her chair. "Where is Hercules? I have eaten far too much and must take a walk."

One of the footmen seemed obviously to be struggling with a desire to speak. Finally, loyalty to his beautiful mistress won out over propriety. "Please, miss, you shouldn't." He cast an anguished look at Henry and, finding a sympathetic eye, continued. "It ain't done. Ladies walking alone."

Fancy laughed merrily. "You mean I can't walk by myself on the street, the street I live on?"

The footman nodded. "Ladies got to have someone along. A gentleman be best if it's in the afternoon. Or a maid in the morning."

Fancy gave the footman a warm smile that made him her slave for life. "Thank you—"

"B-Benson, Miss."

"Thank you, Benson. I appreciate your advice. But I don't set up to be a lady. And I'm much in need of a walk."

Fancy pursed her lovely lips and a shrill whistle echoed through the great house. The scrabble of toenails on wood floors could be heard and in a moment a panting Hercules careened into the room and slid to a crashing halt before his mistress. His great pink tongue lolled wetly from his mouth and from under shaggy clumps of hair two bright eyes peered at her hopefully as his huge tail hit the floor in great thumps.

"Yes, Hercules," said Fancy with a laugh. "We're going for a walk." She scratched behind the great floppy ears, causing Hercules to rub against her in evident joy. "Where is his leash?" she asked.

Henry, with a sigh, fetched it. There was no point, as he well knew, in arguing with Miss Fancy Harper. She had not, as she said, set up to be a lady, and she would certainly not let the opinion of her neighbors keep her from doing exactly as she pleased. And now she pleased to take a walk.

Henry fastened the leash and adjusted the dog's collar. He looked up with a frown. "This collar is fraying, Miss Fancy. Maybe we ought to wait till we get a new one."

"Nonsense, Henry. We'll just have a nice stroll." The green eyes glittered with merriment. "Hercules and I will just take a little promenade around the Square and return home."

Henry inclined his head with a look of a man who knows when he's been bested.

Before the pier glass in the hall, Miss Fancy Harper put on her bonnet. This one was a great huge affair made of straw and tied under her chin with a pale green scarf that seemed somehow to make even more burnished the copper curls that rested against it. She pulled her shawl around her shoulders and extended one slim hand for the leash.

She smiled at Henry. "I shall be perfectly safe,

Henry. Who would risk offending Hercules? Besides," she laughed heartily, "you know how well trained he is."

Henry, a slight smile curving his lips, contented himself with a nod and opened the door for his mistress.

With the great dog pacing sedately at her side, Miss Fancy Harper promenaded the Square. If she was conscious that more than one pair of eyes were watching her from behind curtained windows, she gave no sign of it. For all that she cared St. James's Square might have been a stretch of deserted meadow or upland heath.

Around the square they paced, the great shaggy dog and the lovely young woman. They had almost reached the great house again when the dog stopped suddenly, sniffed the air, gave a sharp bark, and lunged forward. The weakened collar snapped and Fancy was left holding an empty leash.

Whatever words passed her lovely lips at that moment were uttered in a voice too low for any ears but her own. "Hercules!" she commanded. "Come here! Now!"

The great dog paid her no heed, but bounded joyfully off down the street and up the walk to the house to the right of Fancy's, where he threw himself against the door with great enthusiasm.

Muttering under her breath, Fancy followed him. This, she thought with a wry chuckle, was hardly a proper way to meet one's neighbors. She hoped whoever lived in this house would not be unduly perturbed by finding a great brute of a dog flinging himself against the front door.

As she hurried up the walk after the truant, she called out sharply, "Hercules, stop that this instant!"

The dog did stop, but this was not due to Fancy's command but to the fact that the door opened suddenly. In dismay Fancy watched as her dog disappeared into the house.

Then, heaving a sigh, she marched up the steps to be met by a butler whose face appeared carved in granite. Even the generally undismayed Fancy was taken back by the frosty demeanor of this worthy retainer. "My dog," she stammered.

"Will you step inside please, miss?" asked the butler in even tones, his face perfectly composed.

There seemed nothing else to do, so Fancy stepped inside. By this time she was used to living in a great house. But the owner of this house, whoever he was, had decorated it with taste and care—and considerable expense.

She saw that much before a deep voice came from a door to the left. "Phelps! What in the name of heaven is this creature doing in my establishment?"

Through the door, dragging Hercules by the scruff of his neck, came a man. He was tall and dark, with the broad shoulders and long legs of a sportsman—and when he released the dog and straightened to face her, Fancy's hand flew to her mouth in surprise.

"The dog got in unawares, milord," replied Phelps.

"I did not expect that you had *invited* him," said his lordship dryly, cold gray eyes above a scar never leaving Fancy's face. "So," he said. "We meet again."

For a moment Fancy could only stare. Then with a defiant shake of her head she met those gray eyes with her own blazing green ones.

"So it seems," she replied icily. "But certainly through no wish of mine."

William, Earl of Morgane, surveyed her coldly. "I collect *you* are the Bath actress who has taken up residence next door. I feared as much."

Fancy smiled grimly. "I am indeed," said she. "I hope the thought of living next to an actress does not distress you."

Two gray eyes, like pieces of ice, gazed into her own. "As I recall," drawled the Earl with lazy insolence, "I once contemplated living in even closer proximity to an actress."

Fancy flushed, but conscious of the butler, kept back a sharp retort to inquire with sugary sweetness, "I hope your feelings were not too badly hurt when she refused you."

Morgane surveyed her arrogantly. "As I recall the incident, my *feelings* were not the only thing in danger of being hurt."

Fancy knew she was coloring up. What an abominable creature this man was! She had known it at Bath and now she was doubly sure.

As he continued to stare at her sardonically, she felt herself losing her hold on her temper. She had slapped his face once and right now she would dearly love to slap it again.

But she restrained herself. "I have come for my dog. I am sorry if Hercules caused you any trouble."

Morgane lifted a quizzical eyebrow. "Oh, no," said he sardonically. "Huge dogs are accustomed to throwing themselves at my door. I quite enjoy the diversion."

Fancy's anger rose still more. What a terribly arrogant, top-lofty man he was. Just because he was an Earl didn't mean he needed to be so high in the instep. "If my dog has done any damage to your establishment," she said stiffly, "I will pay for it. And now, if you will excuse me —"

As she bent to grab the scruff of Hercules's neck she thought bitterly how chuckleheaded she would look, half bent over, dragging the dog through the street. But she would not ask the haughty Earl of Morgane for so much as the time of day.

"Phelps," said the Earl quietly. "Send someone for some rope and put a temporary collar on this creature."

"Yes, milord."

Fancy, wanting to escape the gaze of those cold gray eyes, was tempted to leave immediately, whether she must drag the dog or no. But common sense asserted itself. If she wanted to stay in the house on St. James's Square—and she did— it would be best not to be on the outs with her neighbors. Though she could never like the man who was still surveying her from lazy gray eyes, she could hope to behave politely toward him. For all her red hair and fiery temper, Fancy was a practical person and she saw no reason to make an implacable enemy out of one who might possibly otherwise remain neutral.

With Phelps gone the two were alone in the hall. "That is very kind of you," Fancy forced herself to say. "Hercules is rather difficult to drag around."

The Earl did not reply to this and Fancy found her resolution to be polite slipping again.

Morgane took a step closer. With difficulty Fancy stood her ground. She was not a small woman, but the Earl towered over her and there was something overpowering in his sheer physical presence.

"I have been known to be *very* kind," he said sarcastically. "As I would have proven to you if I had been given the chance."

Fancy colored up, her eyes glittering. "As I told you then, I am not the kind of woman that you believe I am. I do not need or want a—a protector. I can take care of myself."

The Earl laughed, but no merriment reached his eyes. "So I see. I collect the Marquis was willing to bestow his gifts just for the privilege of gazing on your beauty. The old man was stranger than I thought."

Fancy gaped at this insult. "I did not know the Marquis personally," she cried. "He was a distant cousin on my papa's side. I did nothing whatever to persuade him to leave me his house."

The cold gray eyes slid over Fancy's body, coolly, insolently, lingering where he pleased, and then he spoke dryly. "Perhaps I should have offered you more. A grander establishment might have gained my goal. But that was—let me see—almost a year ago. And you were not so well known, though perhaps just as beautiful."

The Earl came closer still, and Fancy, backing away, found a wall behind her. She set her back against it and glared up at him defiantly. "I told you the truth that day, as I am telling it to you now. No man will ever own me."

That same cold smile curved the Earl's thin lips. "Even, I presume, he who pays for the privilege."

As he took another step nearer, something inside Fancy snapped and she raised her hand to lash out at him. How dare he say such terrible things about her! Untrue things!

Her hand was halfway to his cheek when he caught her wrist in a grip of iron. "No woman slaps my face twice," said his lordship grimly. And he pulled her violently into his arms.

Fancy fought him, but he was quick and his lips had found hers and taken them in a savage bruising kiss before she could escape him.

When he released her, she stood quivering with rage. "You are no gentleman," she cried. "Not in any sense of the word. I hate the very sight of you."

The Earl nodded pleasantly. "And you are no lady, my little bit of muslin."

"I have never set up to be a lady," declared Fancy with scorn. "I am an actress and proud of it. I do my work and I love it. And I certainly do not force my person on those who find me obnoxious."

That she had scored a hit she could tell from the way the scar on his cheek changed color, but his face remained calm and his tone even. "You are an actress," he repeated. "A barque of frailty. Men expect you to be frail."

Fancy drew herself up haughtily. "Their expectations are no concern of mine."

Morgane's dark brows drew together in a frown. "You are in the wrong neighborhood," said he. "You say you do not set up to be a lady. This is a neighborhood for ladies. Why not sell your house and buy a small one in some other part of the city? Retire from the stage, marry some industrious man, and raise a family."

Fancy stared at him. "You are way beyond the line, sir. I do not need any help in planning my life. And if I ever do, I shall take care *not* to consult the likes of you!"

For a moment she thought he might reach for her again and her heart pounded in her throat. But the Earl contented himself with staring at her body until she felt the color flooding her cheeks again.

Fortunately Phelps returned with a piece of rope which he fastened around Hercules's neck in lieu of a collar. "That should serve, milord."

"Very well, Phelps. You may go. I shall accompany our visitor to the door."

"Yes, milord."

Fancy fastened the leash and prodded Hercules to his feet. With a sardonic grin the Earl opened the door. She was halfway down the steps when she heard the words. Spoken in an even tone as they were they still carried a heavy threat. "Get out of St. James's Square. You are not wanted here."

Chapter Two

It took Fancy only a few moments to reach the sanctuary of her house, but it seemed like forever. She would not hurry, not when she could feel the eyes of that terrible man boring into her back.

No, she moved sedately, as though she had not a care in the world. But she was seething and when she reached her own door, she thrust the leash at Henry and said grimly, "I am in a vile temper. Do not speak to me. I'll be in my sitting room. And lock up that monstrous dog. Out of my sight."

Then she marched up the great stairs to the sitting room that she had taken for her own. In front of the cheval glass she yanked off her bonnet and threw it angrily into a chair. "He's a beast," she said aloud. "An absolute beast."

She stomped over to the pitcher and basin,

29

poured in some water, soaped up a rag and scrubbed at her lips till they were numb. The beast, the arrogant top-lofty creature, thought he could run everyone's life.

She stomped through the door and threw herself down on the great mahogany bed, nearly ripping one of the deep green curtains from its hanging. Her hands curled into fists and she pounded the pillow angrily until she was exhausted. Only then did she let the tears come.

Flat on her back she lay, looking up at the canopy of her bed, not really seeing the material there.

Her mind was traveling back in time. To Bath—just about a year ago. That had been her first really good season, the year she was twenty. She had developed well and she knew many parts. How could she avoid it; the daughter of Fanny Harper, born in a dressing room during a performance. The theater was in her blood as it had been in her mama's.

Fancy sighed. She could remember her mama—a dainty little woman with hair the color of Fancy's and great green eyes. Fancy remembered her most often singing as she moved around the rooms that were home.

Even then the young Fancy had badgered and pestered, consumed by her longing for the stage. But Mama had been reluctant to let her act. "You are the daughter of an aristocrat," she told Fancy. "If your papa had not been a younger son, you might have been a lady."

Such might-have-beens held no importance for the youthful Fancy. She could be a lady any time she pleased just by pretending. And Papa didn't seem any different to her than any other man who came to the theater.

But Mama had remained adamant until that terrible day that she took sick and told the eight-year-old Fancy that she should be a good girl and mind her papa because her mama had to go away.

Certainly Fancy had done all she could to be good, but nothing had helped. Before her very eyes Papa had withered away and died, too. Without the woman for whom he had left his high-class life he did not care to live. And so, within six months, Fancy had lost both her parents.

Two great tears stood in her eyes and rolled unheeded down her cheeks. For a while everything in the world had been wrong. Without Henry and Ethel the lost little girl might very well have died, too.

But Henry and Ethel, who had been with Mama and Papa since their marriage, had taken care of her. And the theater had filled the empty place in her life.

So she had grown, and Henry, who was himself an actor, had coached her in her lines, and Fancy Harper had realized her ambition. She had become an actress. Since she was a hard worker and the theater was her life, her parts had grown more and more important, until, at the end of her last season at Bath, an offer had come from the proprietors of Covent Garden. Success was now within her grasp.

From a distant corner of the house came a howl from the disconsolate Hercules. Fancy smiled grimly. That dog deserved to lose his freedom, behaving like that. It was bad enough that he had broken his collar and rushed off to the Earl's house. But then to lie there sleeping contentedly while that haughty lord kissed her!

Fancy had never been so naive as to be unaware of the fringe benefits that lovely young actresses often received from certain lords. But she had not desired such things. And because Henry could not be with her in the dressing room they had trained Hercules to protect her. The moment a man embraced Fancy the great dog was there. Hercules was not unfriendly; he did not even growl. But somehow a big dog putting his paws on a man's shoulders was enough to discourage any amorous thoughts he might be having.

Fancy had always been polite to the lords who offered to set her up in keeping, but she made it clear to them that she had no need of a man. The theater was her love. And if for some reason they refused to believe her, Hercules was there. Except for that once.

Fancy frowned, remembering the night in Bath when the Earl of Morgane had come to her dressing room. Earlier it had been rather crowded with admirers, a situation that Fancy encouraged, feeling that there was safety in numbers.

But later that night when she had shed her costume and emerged from behind the screen in her dress to go home, there had been but two men standing there: a little foppish beau who looked strangely childlike, and the dark-haired stranger, whose scarred cheek gave him a slightly sinister cast.

It was not that, however, that set Fancy's teeth on edge at the very outset. It was the scene that she saw as she emerged from behind the screen. The Earl was staring the fop down and he was being quite successful. The beau turned red, mumbled an apology to Fancy, and scurried out the door like a frightened rabbit.

Fancy found herself alone with a dark man whose gray eyes slid familiarly over her body. He was handsome in a brooding way. Even the scar on his right cheek had a certain charm. He was tall, too, of a height to tower over her. In spite of herself she found she was holding her breath as his eyes continued to rove.

"I hope you have seen enough," she said curtly. She was angry with him. This man had no right to drive away those whose admiration she had earned.

He smiled sardonically. "Actually, I have not," he replied with a dry chuckle. "But I don't suppose you will favor me with anymore."

"Of course not! Who are you anyway?" demanded an irate Fancy.

The stranger gave an elegant bow and smiled

cynically. "I am William, Earl of Morgane, as I'm sure you are quite aware."

"Why should I know you?" replied Fancy angrily. She was rapidly losing control of her temper and she knew it.

The cynical smile did not leave his face. "Because I am one of the wealthiest men in England and I can buy you whatever you want." His eyes were frankly appraising and he nodded. "Yes, you are just as beautiful as I thought."

Fancy stared at the man in amazement. She did not care that he was an Earl. He could be the Prince of Wales himself and she would refuse such an offer.

"I thank you for your compliment, milord, but I believe you have mistaken your woman. I am not for sale."

Morgane laughed. "So you are one of those," he observed sarcastically. "Well, let me tell you, my chit, I am not such a chucklehead as to be rooked out of a fortune by a fancy piece such as yourself." He smiled again, a hateful smug smile. "Quite an appropriate name yours. Prophetic, one might say. But there is no point in playing games with me. I will set you up in a decent establishment, pay your reasonable expenses, give you a piece of fine jewelry from time to time, if you please me. But I expect to be your sole . . . benefactor."

In disbelief Fancy listened to the words. He really believed that she would give herself to him in this cold and heartless way.

34

As he spoke he moved closer and now Fancy realized that his face was only inches from hers. "I believe that I am entitled to sample the wares before I lay down my blunt," said he. For one terrified moment she stared up into those icy gray eyes and then, as she saw his mouth descending toward hers, her reflex was automatic.

The sharp crack of an open palm meeting a cheek echoed in the room. The Earl's expression never changed, but his eyes darkened angrily. "Am I to conclude that you have refused my offer?"

Fancy found herself breathing heavily. "I do not care what you conclude," she cried angrily. "Only leave my dressing room and never come near me again. Never!"

Morgane raised a quizzical eyebrow. "This cannot be the first offer of keeping you have had," he observed harshly. "I advise you not to hold out for too high a price. Even beauty such as yours fades. Too bad. I would have done handsomely by you."

"Out!" cried Fancy, her temper now completely out of control. "Out!"

And when he continued to stare at her arrogantly she grabbed the nearest object at hand, which happened to be a box of powder. She would have thrown it at him, for she was driven past all caring by the cynical amusement in those cool gray eyes and the supercilious curl of his lip. But just as she drew back to hurl the box the door opened to admit Ethel.

Sheepishly Fancy returned the powder box to

the dressing table. The Earl took the opportunity to bow gracefully and leave. But at the door he stopped and turned.

"Perhaps I ought to warn you, Fancy." The intimate way he spoke her name made her long to strangle him. "I am a man who gets what he wants. Even if I have to wait for it."

As the door shut behind him Fancy burst into tears of rage and stamped her feet in frustration, such frustration that it took Ethel many minutes to quiet her.

Indeed, for many weeks after the event she had surreptitiously searched the audience for the sight of that dark sinister face. But the Earl of Morgane never appeared at the theater again. He had left Bath the day after their encounter, Fancy finally learned. And eventually the memory of him had faded from her mind.

But now, she rubbed absently at her bruised lips, now he was right next door. A shiver of fear ran through her as she remembered his parting words that night at the theater. The Earl of Morgane always got what he wanted, did he, she told herself grimly. Well, they would see. He hadn't gotten what he wanted from her before and he wouldn't get it now. Fancy Harper wasn't afraid of any man.

She was going to stay right there, right in the house that her cousin Cavendish had left her. Let the top-lofty Earl see how he liked that!

Suddenly she got up and walked to the cheval

glass. Carefully she studied her features. Many men had told her she was beautiful and she had always taken it for granted that beauty would last, for some time at least. Not for many months had she recalled the Earl's harsh statement that all beauty faded. She scrutinized her face again and gave a sigh of relief; her looks were still good. Besides, when they began to fail and she could no longer play young women she would still be able to play many great roles. Look at Mrs. Siddons. Age had not stopped *her*.

Let the arrogant Earl rant about fading beauty. Fancy Harper would pay him no heed, no heed at all.

She pursed her lips. They seemed a little swollen, a little tender. That brute had bruised them with his savage kiss.

For a moment Fancy closed her eyes. How strong and hard his body had felt against hers. She felt again the tide of anger that had overwhelmed her with his kiss.

Evidently Morgane believed himself a real prime article. No doubt he had been amazed by her refusal of his offer in Bath. But for what reason he should kiss her now, and like that, Fancy couldn't say.

Fancy, who, in spite of Hercules, had been the recipient of many kisses, tried to analyze what it was that made this kiss so different. Generally she laughed at the men who made her offers—laughed goodnaturedly and refused them.

Never had she slapped a man's face before that day—nor had she ever done so since. What was it about the Earl of Morgane that raised such violent emotions in her? With the others she had been gently amused, but with him she had experienced a seething rage. Perhaps it had to do with Morgane's top-lofty attitude. Where the others had begged, supplicated, Morgane assumed her compliance. Yes, it must be that, she told herself, that caused the storm in her insides, that made her want to slap his handsome face yet again. Oh, how it made her pant with suppressed anger when he stood there so insolently, those cool gray eyes raking her body.

Fancy turned from the mirror with an exclamation of disgust. The Earl was far too high in the instep for her taste. And that scar. She shivered slightly at the thought of those cold gray eyes meeting those of his opponents. With those eyes, she told herself grimly, the man would have the edge on anyone. Fancy felt cold just thinking about them, but then she scolded herself. She had never been one to back down from a battle. And she would not do so this time—even if her opponent were the fierce-visaged Morgane.

Fancy sank into a chair. The black unruly hair, the icy gray eyes beneath bushy black brows, the aristocratic nose and thin lips, and on his cheek the scar, white against his dark skin.

Fancy shivered again. There was a lot of power in the man—raw arrogant power. What a good

38

actor he would make, she thought, but of course that was out of the question. Earls did not act upon the stage. This Earl apparently did not even think particularly highly of the theater. He seemed to regard it merely as a marketplace for the acquisition of his latest dasher.

Again Fancy was caught in the memory of that kiss. She should have bit him or stomped on his feet. Anything to keep those lips from meeting hers. Turmoil swept over her at the savage way he had dragged her into his arms. And all the while that miserable Hercules had slept contentedly!

But why had he kissed her like that, almost as a kind of punishment? How terribly insulting the man was. He certainly hadn't improved a bit since that day in Bath when he had reminded her that men often spoke of their dashers as "fancies." Well, she thought, tossing her copper curls disdainfully, let the Earl talk. Talk was cheap and her name was her own.

Mama had given her that name—out of some favorite play long forgotten—and Fancy would never give it up. Never. And certainly not to please the high-flying conceited braggart next door!

Chapter Three

Long before Fancy felt ready for it opening night
was upon her. Actually, her part in *Macbeth* was
very small. It was not until two nights later, when
Cooke, if he appeared, would be playing *Richard
III*, that she would have much of a speaking part.
But Fancy had taken a page from the life of the
great Peg Woffington. Like that mistress of the
stage she would take any part assigned her and do
it to the best of her ability.

But, alighting from her carriage at the stage
door, she was just as excited as she would have
been had she been playing a leading role. The
theater was her life's blood and Fancy reveled in
every aspect of it. In tonight's performance of
Macbeth she would get to see the great John Philip
Kemble and his sister, Mrs. Siddons, perform. Two

of the greats of the English stage. Of course she had seen them rehearse, but this would be her first chance to see them in action—in front of an audience.

Henry had been a little concerned because of rumors of trouble over the new prices, but Fancy had scoffed at him. "You worry too much, Henry. Remember, this is the theater. When the play begins, everything will be all right."

Henry, whose experience of the theater had included more than one riot, had not been convinced by this kind of logic, but said nothing further. The coachman would come after her early and the grooms would be riding along. In this way she should be safe on the journey home.

Fancy quickly put on her makeup and costume and hurried to a place in the wings. She wanted to hear the great Kemble give the occasional address. The theater was full, she saw, especially the pit where dandies and people of other classes were cracking nuts and peeling oranges, throwing the debris at each other cheerfully and bantering gaily. The crowd did not seem unusual. Such things were expected of any audience, just as most of the *ton* would spend their time, after a late entry, in ogling each other.

As the curtain drew up and the stately Kemble stepped upon the stage and began speaking, the theater erupted into noise. Hoots, hisses, catcalls, and shouts of "old prices" made the theater a scene of chaos. Some of the crowd sat with their backs to the stage. Others stood on their benches, hats still on, singing and yelling.

Fancy shivered; the men out there were ugly, really angry. Someone could very well get hurt. Of course she had known about Kemble and the proprietors raising the prices, but she had supposed it was necessary. After all, the old Covent Garden had burnt down last September and it was very expensive to rebuild. And all the actors and actresses had lost their stage costumes, some collected over many, many years and impossible to replace. Too, this new theater was a larger one, very richly decorated. The five tiers of boxes running entirely around the house were supported by slender fluted pillars—and they were gilded. The boxes were highly ornamented and so were the ceilings. The whole thing was supposed to have cost £150,000.

Fancy knew, too, that the new prices were quite high: seven shillings for a box and four shillings for the pit. But could the theater be that important to those ruffians out there, or were they just looking for trouble?

As the play went on the upper gallery grew more and more noisy. A great many soldiers rushed in to capture these rioters, who then let themselves down to the lower gallery and escaped. Fancy could not hear them for the noise in the theater— the cries and shouts created a constant clamor— but Kemble and Mrs. Siddons spoke their lines as though they had the full attention of the house. Their faces never for a second reflected the fact that they were facing a hostile, rioting crowd.

Fancy's heart swelled with pride for them. And when the time came for her to do her bit, she moved onstage and ignored the audience like a trouper. Later, back in the safety of the wings, she had to admit to herself that she was frightened. The crowd was ugly—very ugly.

She had heard about such things, but they had never seemed real to her. In all her years in the theater she had never seen a rioting crowd. It was not only frightening to her physically, but also mentally. It was rather like having someone in your family suddenly go mad. After all, the audience was a vital part of any performance. And noisy and unruly as they often were, Fancy was accustomed to thinking of them as her friends. Now they had become enemies, suddenly vicious enemies. It was very difficult to bear.

And the concern of the rest of the company, most of whom seemed on Kemble's side, was very evident.

So upset was Fancy by the events of the evening that when Henry arrived with two grooms to escort her to her carriage, she had no word of censure for that faithful servant. Indeed, once in the coach she laid her pounding head against his shoulder and whimpered, "Oh, Henry, it was awful. They've gone mad—all of them."

43

Henry spoke the soothing words he knew she wanted to hear. "It'll blow over. You'll see. Things'll be back right afore long."

But even this attempt at comfort was interrupted by the raucous voices of rioters marching down the pavement four and five abreast.

Fancy peered out her window. "They're pushing people into the kennels, Henry! Oh, it's horrible."

"Don't look, Miss Fancy. We're safe enough in here. Come now, we'll be home soon in St. James's Square. There's no call to worry yourself."

True to Henry's word they reached home safely, and as she quitted the carriage Fancy wondered what would happen now. Would they do *Richard III* on the twentieth as advertised?

What a reception Uncle George would get, she thought. Surely he had never faced an audience like that. A little fear nagged at her. She hoped that Uncle George would not have been too liberally at the bottle before his performance. Certainly Mr. Kemble wasn't at all happy that Uncle George had ignored rehearsals.

He was a great actor, George Frederick Cooke, especially good in *Richard III*. And, of course, he was not really her uncle. But he had been a friend of Mama's in the old days and he had kept up his interest in Fancy and her career.

As Ethel helped her weary mistress undress for bed, she too heard about the terrible behavior of the crowd. She clicked her tongue, tucked Fancy into bed like a child, and said, "Don't you be worrying none. They'll probably close down for a while. Ain't no use trying to act for a crowd like that."

But two days later *Richard III* was still scheduled and Fancy insisted that her place was at the theater. This was her chance, she told the worried pair who tried to dissuade her.

"Mr. Kemble hired me and he expects me to be there," she said. "I'm not going to ruin my career because some fools want to riot."

As usual Fancy got her way, but she was not sorry for the two stout grooms or the comforting presence of Henry. "I'll be back to fetch you," he said. "And you just wait in the dressing room till I come for you."

"Yes, Henry. I will. Don't worry yourself now. I'll be all right."

Henry was not too sure of this, but he felt there was little he could do at the moment. And, since he would be there to see her safely home through the mob, he was satisfied.

Fancy hurried into makeup and costume and went looking for Uncle George. She had not found it surprising that he hadn't come to the house on St. James's Square even though she had sent him a letter telling him all about it. For one thing he may well have not had the money to pay for the letter's delivery. Or he may have read it and then forgotten it. When he was bosky, Uncle George had a very poor memory, as she well knew. Or he may have not wanted to come into the neighborhood of the *haut ton*.

But, at any rate, she *had* let him know of her good fortune and she looked forward to seeing him. She had not even been particularly surprised to find that he ignored rehearsals. An actor of his caliber could well do that. But she hoped that this night, at least, he would not be in his cups.

Or, if he were, that the boxkeeper, John Brandon, had succeeded in "doctoring" him up. Fancy had heard Mr. Kemble remark, in a tone of gratitude, that, without Brandon, Cooke would have failed to take his place on stage much more often.

It was difficult enough for a sober man to face that horrible crowd, but for one in his altitudes— Fancy frowned as she made her way toward the men's dressing rooms.

A knock on the door brought another actor who replied that Cooke would meet her in the greenroom shortly. So Fancy, her anxiety still unrelieved, made her way to the greenroom and paced restlessly through the empty room. Once she stopped to survey herself in the great gilded mirror, but the face and figure that looked back at her showed no sign of aging. She wrinkled up her nose and announced pertly, "So much for you, milord."

A hearty laugh from the doorway made her turn. There stood Cooke in costume for Richard. "Uncle George!" cried Fancy, and raced across the room to throw herself into his open arms.

46

In a moment he held her off. "Come, come, a great hulking girl like you has no business in the arms of an old rogue like me."

"Uncle George," protested Fancy. "You are being silly. Did you get my letter?"

Cooke nodded. "Of course I did. Glad to hear of your good fortune. Wager the neighbors are not, though."

Fancy managed a little laugh. "Actually they are not bad. The ladies cut me on the street, but the gentlemen are quite kind."

Cooke snorted. "I expect so. A beauty like you." He frowned at her. "I trust you've remained a good girl."

"Uncle George!" Fancy flushed. "You know I have no taste for men."

Cooke ran a hand through his dark hair. "You're human, m'girl. Remember that. It's just that beauty like yours ought to get a good price."

Fancy flushed again. "Uncle George, you make me sound like a piece of merchandise." She was very much aware of the odor of rum on his breath, but his eyes seemed all right.

"You'd best take a sensible view of the world, Fancy, m'girl. There are those with beauty and those willing to buy it. We've each got to use what gifts we have."

Fancy shook her head. "You mistake me, Uncle George. I do not intend to marry or—or anything else. The theater is my life."

Cooke shook his head. "For now, m'dear. But

47

there'll be a man; I don't doubt it. For you've your mama's blood in you."

Fancy dropped her eyes in confusion. She had always suspected that Uncle George had loved Mama in those long ago days before she had met Papa. And perhaps Mama had even cared for him —though not in the same way she loved Papa. But there was no opportunity for her to say more for the greenroom began to fill up with players, all talking to each other in an effort to keep up their spirits, and she knew that the curtain would soon go up.

Fancy, watching Uncle George laugh and joke with the others, knew that in a few moments, when he moved onto the stage, he would become an evil, dissimulating man, bent and deformed. And that deformity would not be indicated just by the padded hump on his back, but by the very cast of his features.

And she herself, when she faced him as Lady Anne, widow of the Edward he had murdered, would be entirely that Anne. There, on the stage, in the magic of the footlights, Fancy and Uncle George would cease to exist and there would be only the beautiful young woman and the evil, cunning Richard whose wily words so appealed to her vanity that she would finally consent to become wife to a man she had every cause to hate and despise.

As everyone scurried to their places, ready for the first act, Fancy felt her heart beating in her throat. The crowd out there was ugly, just as ugly as the one last night and the night before. And Uncle George had had quite a bit to drink. If he should get angry at them for refusing to listen—a shudder ran over Fancy. Then she scolded herself. Uncle George was a veteran of the stage. Nothing would shake his sense of presence.

As the curtain went up on the scene of a London street, Fancy watched Cooke become the wicked hunchback and enter to impart to the audience his evil machinations. They greeted him first with applause, to indicate that their quarrel was not with him but with Kemble. And then they began to hiss, "Off! Off!"

Not a word that Cooke spoke reached their ears. Groans and catcalls resounded throughout the house. Banners and placards were everywhere evident. Fancy caught her breath as she read one which had just been hoisted.

COOKE DESERVES OUR PITY.
KEMBLE OUR CONTEMPT.

Fancy held her breath. If Cooke got his back up, he might let go at the audience. But as the act continued she slowly released her breath. Uncle George seemed oblivious to the audience. They did not exist for him. And shortly, when it came her turn to go on, Fancy, too, was able to ignore the disturbances out front.

After Richard and Anne had exchanged insults

49

and the cunning Richard had given the lady the opportunity to kill him, an opportunity he knew she would not be able to avail herself of, when she had spit upon him and been beguiled, and finally, left her place in the mourning procession of Henry VI and exited to wait at Crosby House for the pseudopenitent Richard, Fancy stood again in the wings, exhausted. Her first big scene in London was over. And no one had even heard it.

The play progressed, the catcalls and groans, hoots and hisses, never abating. Now and then a post horn echoed through the house and then suddenly the theater was full of pigeons, flying distractedly, landing here and there in confusion.

Between acts Fancy met Uncle George coming back from his dressing room and the unnatural shine in his eyes told her plainly that he had been at his bottle. She really could not blame him. That audience was a horror to face and he was on stage almost constantly. That had to be very tiring. But the gin, or whatever it was, that Uncle George had been sampling, would not help. And Fancy knew from experience that Cooke might be doing his part perfectly, even when under the influence, and then, very suddenly snap and begin to harangue the audience in the lewdest of language. Such conduct could be very dangerous with a crowd like this.

Though her first scene was her big one and she would not need to appear again for some time, Fancy continued to wait in the wings, watching.

The second act had barely begun when from one of the boxes came the voice of a man. The crowd hushed to listen. Fancy recognized the man as a lawyer, one of the lawyer kind, as Henry would say. He launched into a great tirade, alternating abuse of Kemble and Siddons with allusions to Catalani and others. The British stage should not be contaminated by Italian depravity and French duplicity, he said.

Fancy could hardly believe her ears. Surely the rioters could not blame a performer for seeking the best salary possible. Other placards were hoisted.

MOUNTAINS AND DICKENS, NO CATS NO KITTENS.

Placards and banners hung everywhere over the boxes. One sign announced that together the Kembles and Madame Catalani would that season earn £25,575. Certainly, thought Fancy, that *was* an awful lot. But Kemble and Mrs. Siddons were greats; they had been many years in the theater. And everyone knew that Madame Catalani, great singer that she was, was all the rage in London.

Fancy had not noticed any change in the level of noise from the audience and orange peels, nut shells, apple cores, and other such refuse that had been hitting the stage from time to time, when suddenly Cooke whirled and faced the audience.

Fancy caught her breath. It had happened! Something had precipitated it and Uncle George had cast aside his role and was going to give his tormentors a dressing down. He advanced right to the edge of the stage, and, as Fancy watched, his shoulders went back and he raised his fist. The clamor in the pit grew louder and more paper and orange peels came sailing through the air.

And then Fancy saw what Cooke, intent on a specific part of the audience, did not. A band of ruffians was advancing and had almost reached the orchestra. As they pushed aside the musicians, Fancy flew onto the stage. Desperately she pulled at the irate Cooke who was thundering out tremendous lewd oaths and threatening the audience with every known obscenity.

"Uncle George," she cried. "Please!" But her words could not be heard over the tumult; and then, just as the rioters reached the stage, Cooke turned and pushed away what he apparently thought was another rioter.

Fancy, knocked from her feet by the force of his blow, saw the expression of chagrin on his face as he recognized what he had done. And then the terror hit her; for she fell into the arms of the rioters, who, shouting loudly, began to bear her back into the pit.

Fancy fought her panic. These were dangerous men, highly wrought up, who thought it a great joke to pass her struggling body back and forth high in the air above their heads. And, suspended as she was, to struggle was only to increase her danger.

She was losing her battle with panic, however,

for if they decided to continue on out of the theater she could expect little mercy at the hands of such men. Suddenly the cries and shouts changed their tone. The rioters beneath her began to break and run. Those in front stopped suddenly as though facing an obstacle. For a moment those who held Fancy aloft hesitated. As the room slowed its whirling she had a glimpse of a dark scarred face and a laughing fair one. And suddenly the ground came up to meet her. She felt her head strike something hard and then there was nothing but darkness.

Slowly Fancy fought her way up out of the darkness. It was comfortable there, cool and safe. She did not want to leave it. But insistently something kept pulling her back to consciousness. Finally she realized that someone was repeating her name. "Fancy, Fancy," he was saying. And then there was something cool on her forehead. It was strange about that voice, she thought dreamily. She had heard it before, surely she had. But now the tone of it was different, softer, caring.

Slowly she opened her eyes. She was lying on the stage, she saw, and someone had put something soft under her head to cushion it. She felt a button pressing against her neck.

"That's better," said the same voice, now in a gruffer tone. Slowly Fancy turned her head and met the dark sardonic eyes of the Earl of Morgane. He knelt beside her, one hand on the cloth that lay on her brow. Slowly Fancy's brain took in the fact that he was coatless. His coat! It was his coat

53

under her head. She made a movement to rise and was unceremoniously thrust down again.

"Just a moment, hothead," said Morgane. "You've taken quite a crack on that thick skull of yours. Now lie still."

Beside Morgane's face appeared the fair one she had glimpsed earlier. "Who—?" She tried to form the words with dry lips.

"Castleford," said the fair face, smiling grimly. "Friend of Morgane's here. Lucky for you he was in the audience."

"How—?" began Fancy again.

"We just faced the ruffians down," said Castleford cheerfully. "They were only a bunch of cowards. Morgane here could have done it alone. I just went along for the lark."

"Thank you," said Fancy, her eyes moving back to Morgane.

He shrugged. "You behaved very foolishly."

Fancy, now that her strength was returning, was beginning to feel her usual irritation with this arrogant man. "I was trying to warn Uncle George," she protested.

"*Uncle* George?" said Morgane sarcastically.

Fancy wished she had her strength back; she longed to slap his handsome face.

"He was Mama's friend. I have always called him uncle."

"He's a fool," observed his lordship curtly. "An audience like that can't be reasoned with and

54

should certainly never be threatened. If Kemble doesn't lower the prices, this theater is doomed."

Fancy struggled once more to sit up. This time Morgane helped her, one strong arm supporting her back. The room whirled briefly and then righted itself.

Suddenly Cooke appeared. He looked extremely humble as he knelt beside her. "Fancy, m'girl, I'm so sorry. I didn't know it was you."

"I know, Uncle George. I'm all right, really I am. Don't you fuss yourself." She looked around her, suddenly realizing how quiet it was. "What happened to the rest of the play?"

"We said we could not continue," replied Kemble, whom Fancy now saw standing to one side. "And with you lying here unconscious most of the crowd was anxious to leave."

Fancy raised her hand to her throbbing head.

"How do you feel?" asked Morgane, still in that curt voice.

But Fancy was too exhausted to bristle up. "I am rather lightheaded," she said. "And my head aches horribly."

"You had a vicious bump," observed Castleford. "Wonder it didn't knock all your brains out."

This remark earned him a dark look from his friend. "What you need is a little stimulant." Morgane gave Cooke a glance. "Is there anything left in that bottle of yours?"

Fancy saw Cooke color up, but if he thought of

sharp retort, he kept it to himself and hurried off, returning in a minute with a flask which he offered to Morgane.

"I don't want any—" began Fancy, only to be silenced by a look from the Earl.

"Stop behaving like an obnoxious child and take a swallow. You have certainly caused the company enough trouble already."

"I?" sputtered Fancy, gazing up into the dark face so near her own.

"Yes, you. There was no need for such heroics. Cooke can hold his own with any audience and at least if they had carried him off he would not have been in the sort of danger that threatened you."

Fancy colored up again. "I am dreadfully sorry to have caused you so much inconvenience, milord," she replied icily. "But I did not *ask* you to come to my rescue."

"Perhaps not," observed he dryly. "But, connoisseur of beauty that I am, I did not wish to discover your beautiful body lying somewhere in the kennels outside."

Fancy could not repress a shudder. Mobs could do things like that. She was about to offer the Earl a somewhat stilted apology when he put the flask to her lips. It was either drink or have rum splashed relentlessly down the front of her costume. Fancy swallowed and coughed as the fiery liquid hit her stomach.

Morgane returned the flask to Cooke, who accepted it sheepishly. Then the Earl cast his dark gaze on the rest of the company, still gathered around. "I believe Miss Harper is sufficiently recovered to be taken to the dressing room. Castleford, kindly bring my coat."

And before Fancy could even think, the Earl was on his feet and had lifted her easily into his arms. "I can walk," she cried angrily, as he began to move off stage.

"Quite probably," he returned, unperturbed. "But I do not intend that you should. And it would be of considerable help to me, since you are not exactly of sylphlike proportions, if you could so conquer your aversion to me as to manage to assist me by putting your arms around my neck."

Fancy, mindful of the others watching and aware of her own lightheadedness, reluctantly did as she was told. His shirt was cool under her fingers and as her hands met behind his neck she felt them brushed by his dark hair. A strange feeling shot through her as she became aware of the feel of his arms around her and, as the room began to whirl once more, she closed her eyes with a sigh and leaned her head against his shoulder.

Thus he carried her to the dressing room where, banishing the others with another dark look, he carried her inside and set her carefully on her feet, keeping his hands on her elbows to support her. "Now, we will see if you can stand."

Fancy, alone with only this dark man and his friend Castleford, felt a little tremor of fear. There was so much power in the Earl—raw, arrogant

57

power. He was used to having his way—about everything. And she had twice defied him. Once when she refused his offer of keeping and just lately when he had urged her to leave St. James's Square.

She forced her eyes to meet his and was aware that she swayed slightly. "If you will release my elbows, I will see."

With a lazy smile the Earl took his hands away. Slowly, Fancy, putting each foot down carefully, paced the length of the room and back. "I am fully recovered now," she said politely. "And I thank you for your services."

"Your thanks are accepted," replied Morgane laconically, "but my services are not ended."

As her perplexed expression revealed her bewilderment, he chuckled dryly. "I do not propose to drive off and leave you here. Since we are going in the same direction I shall drop you at your door and thus be assured that you are safe. For one night at least."

Fancy drew herself up. The thought of a carriage ride in the company of the dark Earl was almost as terrifying as a rioting crowd, but she would not let him see that. "My man, Henry, will be here for me with two grooms, so I will not need your kind escort."

For a moment the Earl scowled. "I believe I shall just wait around until the redoubtable Henry arrives and thus assure myself of your safety."

"Milord," said Fancy. "I really do appreciate

58

your concern on my behalf. But I am a grown woman, perfectly capable of managing my own affairs."

Morgane laughed, a deep humorless laugh. "You are a foolish chit," he declared. "Who knows little of life and who thinks herself enamored of an illusory phantom called the theater."

Fancy bristled. "Perhaps so, milord, but my love is at least genuine, not induced by rich establishments and fabulous jewels."

"*Touché*," cried Castleford, who had been witnessing this exchange of barbs with great concentration.

Morgane ignored his friend. "Why can't you behave like a sensible woman? Sell that big house, find yourself a decent husband, and raise a family. You are not meant for the theater."

"You are wrong," cried Fancy, forgetting her throbbing head in a rush of anger. "The theater *is* my life. I will *not* give it up. Not you or all the rioters in the world can make me."

"As I said," replied Morgane, smiling darkly, "you *are* a fool."

Fancy, whose fingers had again come to rest on the powder box, fought down the urge to hurl it at this infuriating man. She would not give him that satisfaction.

"If you will excuse me for a moment," said the Earl, reaching for his coat. He shrugged into it and in spite of its having been folded and lain on, it showed hardly a wrinkle. It was cut so well that it clung to each muscle and curve and wrinkles were, perforce, stretched out.

The Earl returned his attention to Fancy. "I imagine that Henry will be here soon. Therefore I propose that Castleford and myself wait outside while you change." His eyes met hers. "Thus not offending your maidenly modesty."

Fancy's fingers closed once more around the powder box, but Morgane, letting his gaze linger there, remarked sardonically, "That would certainly be a peculiar mode of repayment for your rescue. But should the fancy move you, my dear, feel free to hurl it at me. I have never been one to stand in the way of a lady's pleasure."

And the Earl and his friend leisurely stepped out, closing the door behind them.

For a few moments Fancy's fingers trembled so that she was unable to undo the costume, but finally she managed and struggled into her own clothes. As she settled before the mirror to remove her makeup, she scowled at the reflection there. Two great green eyes stared back at her out of a face white as flour. She looked just ghastly, Fancy thought angrily, as she scrubbed away.

Finally she surveyed herself in the mirror. She did not want to face the top-lofty Earl again, but neither did she want to remain alone in the dressing room. And so she moved hesitantly to the door and steeled herself to meet those lazy gray eyes.

But it was not the Earl's lean figure that stood there, but Henry's familiar one. With a cry of relief, she collapsed against him. "Oh, Henry, please take me home."

Chapter Four

The next morning found Fancy in much better spirits. She was really none the worse for her experience. She did notice several bruises on her upper arms but they were minor matters, not worth fussing over. The terror of the night before had already started to fade. And, after all, Fancy had made the theater her life. One bad experience would not turn her against it.

She said this to Ethel very plainly as she breakfasted on the substantial plate of ham, muffins, eggs, and sipped her tea. "You cannot expect me to give up my life's work," she insisted, "simply because some foolish men want to riot."

"It ain't safe," replied Ethel sourly. "You might get pulled off the stage again and this time there wouldn't be no Earl there to save you."

Fancy wrinkled her nose. "The Earl of Morgane is far too high in the instep. He needs taken down."

Ethel shook her head dolefully. "No good comes from mixing with them quality folks. They's different somehow." From Ethel's glum expression it was evident that she did not find the difference to her liking.

Fancy's laughter rang out. "Oh, Ethel. They're not that bad."

"Humph! Haven't none of 'em been to see you, have they? Or even spoke to you on the street?"

Fancy's eyes danced. "The gentlemen have been very kind. They always nod when we pass."

"Humph!" repeated Ethel. "Gentlemen, indeed. They all got an eye for one thing. You mark my words. It was a bad day when we come to St. James's Square. A bad day all around."

Fancy, seeing the Earl of Morgane's scarred face flash before her eyes, shivered. Certainly the Earl was not the sort one would wish for an enemy. He looked positively sinister with that scar and those mocking gray eyes.

"Never mind, Ethel. We'll be happy here. And if the neighbors don't accept us—that's their loss."

She pushed herself back from the table and smoothed down the gown of green-sprigged muslin that clung to her shapely figure. Though not a single soul had come to call in the several weeks they had lived in St. James's Square, Fancy always dressed as though they might. "Where is Hercules?" she asked.

"He's around here somewheres," replied Ethel, her hands flying to her ears as Fancy pursed her lips in a shrill whistle that caused more than one of the smart young footmen to shift nervously at his station.

From a distant part of the house a clatter could be heard approaching and then Hercules slid to a halt only inches from a pedestal that held an expensive vase. Ethel shook her head. "That dog don't belong in no house. He's a sheep dog, he is. Ought to be outside somewheres minding sheep instead of eating us out of house and home."

"Now, Ethel." Fancy patted the great dog's shaggy head. "You know he has always earned his keep. It's just that Mr. Kemble doesn't think I need him backstage now."

Hercules's eyes, behind their screen of shaggy brown and white hair, peered at each of them in turn as if asking for an explanation of the whistle. His great tail thumped the floor happily, to the imminent danger of the vase.

"Come, Hercules," said Fancy. "I'm going to study my lines in the sitting room and you shall keep me company."

Hercules, with a fond look at the doors that led outside, obediently followed her, and as she settled in a chair with the script the dog plopped himself at her feet with a sigh of reproach.

Fancy scowled at him. "You silly dog, you needn't look at me like that. I didn't tell you to go running off to the Earl's house in that stupid fashion. What did you want anyway?"

In answer to this query Hercules merely opened one eye momentarily and then closed it again. Fancy laughed. The dog assuredly felt put upon because he was forced to remain indoors. But *she* was the one who had had to face the supercilious Earl.

What a shame, she found herself thinking, that he was so excessively arrogant and top-lofty. Even with that scar he was a very good-looking man— broad in the shoulders and lean in the hips. Every bit a man. If he had a better temper any woman would be pleased—

Fancy caught herself and frowned. How absolutely ridiculous. To be thinking such thoughts about a man. And such a man. Besides, his temper *was* the vilest, and he was intolerably overbearing. No woman in her right mind would form a partiality for such a creature.

With this settled, she picked up her script and began to study her lines. This was an off day for her since she did not appear in tonight's performance and she must make the most of it. No time for sitting around thinking about a man who had rescued her and then scolded her like she was the merest chit.

Fancy was pacing the floor sometime later, repeating her lines for Morton's *School of Reform,* when the door knocker was heard. It was such an unusual sound that Fancy stopped in her tracks. It hardly seemed possible that someone would be coming to call. Yet assuredly someone *had* knocked.

She found herself standing immobile, holding her breath, until she heard Henry say, "This way, milord."

Then the script began to rustle in her trembling fingers. What lord could be calling on her? She knew no lords except— Her heart seemed to flutter up into her throat.

Then Henry was opening the door to the sitting room. "The Marquis of Castleford to see you, miss."

Fancy knew that Henry was carefully keeping all expression from his face, but something glittered in his eyes. "Thank you, Henry. Please show him in."

As Lord Castleford entered the room, Fancy put the script on a table and turned. "Lord Castleford, how kind of you to call."

The big blond man advanced swiftly and took her hands in his. "Miss Harper, how kind of you to receive me."

Hercules opened one eye, perceived that all was well, and shut it again.

Castleford kept Fancy's hands in his for a long moment while he scanned her face. "You do not appear any the worse for the ordeal of last night."

Fancy managed to pull her hands free. "Thanks to you I am not," she declared, turning toward a chair and inviting him to do likewise.

Castleford pulled his chair close to hers. "You give me too much credit," he said warmly. "It was Morgane that moved first, not I. And it was he who stared the mob down."

The big man laughed, a hearty sound that fell pleasantly on Fancy's ears. "It was the scar that did it, I collect. He can look sinister, can Morgane, but he has a heart of gold."

Fancy's amazement must have been revealed on her face for Castleford laughed again. "I know Morgane doesn't look like he has a heart at all, but he does. I should know; for we grew up together, we did. And he always looked out for me. I was a bumbling boy. Always in the suds. But he fished me out every time. A man never had a better friend."

Fancy, listening to this eulogy in surprise, could only suppose that the Earl's relationships with men were conducted on a very different level than those with women. But she supposed that that was possible. She was about to say so when Castleford made a motion of regret.

"Here I came to inquire about your health after last night's ordeal and instead I go meandering on about nothing. You must excuse me. I believe your beauty has gone to my head and damaged my brains."

Fancy laughed. The Marquis was at least entertaining and he was the first visitor she had had. Besides, it *was* kind of him to inquire about her health.

"I am really quite well," she returned. "The theater is my life, you see, and I will not let one little incident mar my pleasure in it."

Castleford looked around him. "Have you never thought of giving up the theater?"

Fancy scowled. "I have not," she said sharply. "And if your friend sent you here to suggest such a thing, you can just tell him that he's wasting his time."

The Marquis looked at her with the bewildered blue eyes of a baby whose fingers have been slapped for some reason unknown to him. "Morgane doesn't even know I'm here," he said, smiling somewhat sheepishly. "I doubt he would much like it."

"Does the Earl have the right to order your calls?" inquired Fancy curiously.

"Of course not." Castleford looked slightly uncomfortable. "The only thing is—well, he may not like my poaching on his preserves."

For a moment Fancy did not understand. "Poaching?"

"Well—" The Marquis's face turned rosy. "He seems to have pretty well staked out his territory and I wouldn't want to interfere."

Fancy raised an eyebrow. "I believe you are laboring under a misapprehension, milord. The Earl has absolutely no claim on me—now or ever. I am a free agent."

Castleford smiled sheepishly. "I'm very glad to hear that. So now I have a clear field."

"I have no interest in men," said Fancy bluntly. "Nor in being kept."

Castleford flushed again. "Afraid I'm most inept at these things. Never went after a dasher like you before. That is—"

Fancy's gay laughter rang out. "I am *not* a dasher," she said. "But let us forget that. Tell me some more about your childhood."

Castleford grinned. "It was all as I told you. Me constantly in the suds and Morgane pulling me out. We did the Grand Tour together. Only eighteen we were. That's when he got the scar."

"I suppose it was the fault of his horrible temper," observed Fancy with just a touch of smugness.

Castleford stared at her in surprise. "Sometimes I doubt we're talking about the same man. Morgane's as even-tempered as they come."

It was Fancy's turn to stare. How could such a thing be possible? "Well," she insisted, "I'm sure the duel was his fault anyway."

Castleford shook his blond head. "Not at all. Actually Morgane behaved quite handsomely."

"What happened?" In spite of herself Fancy was intrigued. Ethel had reported to her the story that the Earl had killed a man, but the particulars had not been available.

Castleford shook his head. "It wasn't Morgane's fault, I assure you, Miss Harper." A faraway look came into his eyes. "We were a couple of brash young bucks, eager to see the world. And we'd done France and Italy. We decided to spend some time in Germany—Heidelberg. Morgane was always a favorite with the ladies. This particular young lady was the daughter of a Graf. We met her at a supper party."

He sighed. "She was a pert young thing—small, with great round green eyes under deep lashes and a sweet little pink mouth. I could understand Morgane's attraction to the girl. But her father was upset. He wasn't going to have *his* daughter marry a bloody Englishman, Earl or no."

Fancy listened in fascination.

"It seems there was a fiancé in the background, an older type, a man who had made dueling his life. He manufactured an insult in order to call Morgane out. No one consulted the chit, who disappeared from the city. The saber, *Schläger*, they called it, was the thing then and lucky for Morgane he'd always favored the weapon. The fiancé, who had killed half a dozen at least, thought to make short work of him and early on caught him on the cheek. But Morgane wouldn't concede and the other man meant to have another killing."

Fancy found herself on the edge of her chair, her hands clenched into fists, almost as though the outcome of the duel was still in doubt.

"Morgane kept at him till the other man lost his wind. But the death blow wasn't intended. He only wanted to wound his man and make him stop fighting. Afterward, the girl's father set some ruffians on us. Morgane tried to reach the girl. He wanted to bring her with us, make her his wife, and all that. But she wouldn't even see him. Sent word by her maid that he had forfeited her regard. Never saw a man so put down. Thought maybe the wound and that would finish him before his time. Especially since we had to get out of Germany in a hurry.

"But he pulled through. Physically, anyway. And ever since he's been a ladies' man of the first water."

Fancy unclenched her fists and relaxed in the chair. So that was how he got the scar on his face.

She smiled at Castleford. "Have you ever dueled since?"

The big man shook his head. "I stood up with him that day and that was enough. It'll be a good day when Englishmen stop such doings. Pistols are even worse than sabers to my way of thinking—as there's less of skill and more of chance involved."

Fancy was still enthralled by the romantic tale she had heard. "And so he never heard from the girl again?"

Castleford nodded. "Don't know how he would have behaved if he had. He was nutty on that chit. That's for certain."

Fancy could hardly imagine the arrogant Earl so far forgetting himself as to be nutty over any woman. Not that he could not experience desire. Clearly she had seen that glittering in his eyes, felt it in the grip of his hands, been attacked by it in that savage kiss. But, she opined, for all his good looks and charm, the Earl knew nothing of love.

"You must have led a very exciting life," remarked Fancy.

Castleford shrugged. "We have had a lot of adventures, gamed for high stakes, fought with Nelson—both of us at Trafalgar—raced some bang-up teams, and known some beautiful frail ones. But now I'm getting ready to settle down. When a man's reached two and thirty, he begins to think of marriage, of leaving behind his salad days, and devoting himself to his family."

Such a picture of the Earl caused laughter to bubble in Fancy's throat. That one would never settle down. A small giggle escaped her. "You sound like two and thirty is ancient."

Castleford regarded her reproachfully. "You may laugh now in the fullness of your youth," said he. "But I assure you, after thirty a man's thoughts turn to family."

Fancy did not like the direction in which the conversation was going. She rose from her chair. "It was very kind of you to call to inquire after my health," she told him, extending a hand. "I truly appreciate it. But I do not want to keep you from making your other calls. And—since I'm a working woman, I have lines to study."

The Marquis rose and came toward her. Before she knew quite what had happened he had taken her in his arms and was kissing her. Fancy did not struggle, nor did she respond. She simply remained waiting until two great shaggy paws appeared on Castleford's shoulders and a big wet tongue caressed his ear.

The Marquis put her away from him and turned to get the dog off his back. Fancy laughed. "I'm sorry, milord, if Hercules scared you. But he doesn't like my callers to take liberties with my person."

Castleford, appearing considerably shaken by this unusual turn of events, changed color and began to mutter an apology.

"There's no need, milord," said Fancy brightly. "Most men make the assumption you did. But, you see, I am not like most actresses." She glanced around the room. "Thanks to my cousin, Cavendish, I am in no need of a—protector. And, since the theater is the love of my life, I have little need of a man."

The Marquis, seeing that he had not offended her, brightened. "Hope you won't hold it against me," he muttered. "Won't happen again."

Fancy went with him to the door. "It was most kind of you to call," she said, casting a quick glance at a glowering Ethel. "Do come again."

"Oh, I shall. Never fear." And with these words Castleford took his amberheaded cane and gloves, clapped his fawn-colored beaver on his curly locks, and made his escape to the waiting carriage.

73

As the door closed behind him, Fancy turned to Ethel with a smile. "Now we have had our first caller."

Ethel shrugged. "When a lady comes calling, that's the time to get excited. Won't no ladies come calling here."

Fancy shook her copper curls. "That doesn't signify at all, Ethel. Ladies are rather dull company anyway."

This remark elicited a snort and Ethel returned to her duties without further discussion.

As she made her way slowly back to the sitting room, Fancy's brow furrowed in puzzlement. Imagine Morgane being young and in love. It seemed highly impossible. Try as she might she could not imagine the Earl showing tenderness to any woman. He was all passion—fiery temper and savage kisses. Fancy shivered at the memory of that kiss, at the brash arrogance of it.

Well, let the Earl think he was a prime article, Fancy told herself as she picked up her script again. There was no need for her to believe it. And indeed, she would not think about him anymore at all. He was not worth the trouble.

Chapter Five

In spite of her good intentions Fancy found her thoughts straying far too often to the strange man next door. Still, when it was time to dress for dinner, she felt that she had made reasonable progress in learning her new part.

"You behave yourself," she said to the dog, as she rose to leave the room. Hercules raised an eyelid and peered at her before going back to sleep.

As Fancy made her way upstairs, she found her thoughts again reverting to the man next door. He must always have had his way in things, she thought. Witness that arrogant manner of his. Well, she would show him that Earl or no he couldn't run *her* life.

As she slid into a simply cut gown of pale orange jaconet, Fancy's mind went again over the story of the Earl's youthful duel. In her imagination she tried to picture him young and unscarred, those cool gray eyes following some young woman with love and longing. But her imagination simply would not cooperate. She could only envision him with eyes like bits of gray ice, with those thin lips that curled scornfully, with that scar that reflected his anger when nothing else did. With a sigh, Fancy ran the brush through her copper curls. She simply must get that horrible man out of her thoughts.

Minutes later she was being seated at the dining room table. In spite of all her protestations to the contrary Ethel and Henry had refused to be treated as the equals and friends that she regarded them. "It ain't fitting," was Ethel's sole comment.

And Henry echoed it. "You must see, Fancy, child," he had said to her in the tone he had used when she was a little one, "I can't keep order and such and run this establishment proper if I do that."

And Fancy had been forced to nod in agreement. So now she sat in solitary state while the footmen stood by. It was all really bird-witted to her way of thinking, but if that's what Henry wanted, if it made his work easier, she would do it.

She had just finished a fine meal, topped off with a portion of apple tart, and was sighing in contentment, when suddenly there came a loud knocking on the door. There was something loud and arrogant about the knock itself, almost as if—

Fancy rose hastily, dropping her napkin. It couldn't be.

"Oh, dear," she heard Henry say. "I'm most sorry, milord. I don't know how he got out."

"I wish to speak to your mistress," said the deep voice she knew so well. "I cannot be spending all my time dragging this brute home."

Fancy felt herself bristling up. He needn't be so high and mighty about things. She straightened her back and moved out to meet him. "Milord," she said, as graciously as she could manage.

His cool gray eyes raked her body before they settled on her face. "So, Miss Harper. I find that you are not being a good neighbor."

"Milord!" Henry began, but Fancy silenced him with a look.

"If you please, milord," said Fancy quite calmly, "let us continue this conversation in the drawing room."

The Earl's lip curled cynically. "If you so desire," he said curtly.

As Fancy led the way to the drawing room, she was extremely conscious of the Earl's eyes on her back. The man made her nervous. Not even a full house had the capacity of this haughty lord to make her conscious of every movement she made.

Fancy closed the door behind him and motioned him to a chair. The Earl remained standing. "I am flattered," he drawled, "that you wish to be alone with me."

Fancy felt herself coloring up. "I merely wish to

keep your angry remarks from resounding throughout my household," she replied curtly.

"Ah," said he, eyeing her speculatively. "You expect me to be angry."

Fancy was taken aback. "Of course. That is—you have every right." She stopped, aware that his eyes were glittering with suppressed amusement.

"I believe I shall baffle your expectations," he drawled. "I shall be the soul of affability."

For a long moment Fancy stared in amazement. Now what was the man up to? "I—I find this affability difficult to countenance," she faltered. "Why not say your piece about the dog? Vent your anger and leave?"

"I am not angry," said the Earl, regarding her carefully. "That dog is really a rare creature. It gives me a great deal of pleasure to hear him throw himself against my new mahogany door. He assures me that the door is sound and provides me protection against robbers and such."

This statement was made in the soberest of tones and Fancy was at a loss as to how to respond. "I am sorry about Hercules," she said. "I don't know why he always wants to come to your house. I can't understand it. He's never been a dog to run away."

The Earl shrugged. "Perhaps he enjoys my company. Some people do."

Fancy glanced at him sharply, but he was regarding her quite urbanely. If he had laughed in that sardonic way of his or if he had been angrily insulting, she could have let loose her own anger. But how could she round on a man who now was making himself so affable?

As she watched he settled into a chair and stretched his long, well-clad legs comfortably. For a moment Fancy hesitated. Then she, too, seated herself.

For long moments there was silence in the room. The Earl seemed extremely comfortable. He looked around him with interest. "Old Cavendish did you up well. I rather imagine this is a Robert Adam house."

Fancy looked at him in surprise. Whatever was the man talking about now?

"Robert Adam," said the Earl, as though patiently instructing a child, "was a great architect of the last century. He built a great many houses, including mine. The detail of the carving in the panel over the fireplace, for instance, is quite reminiscent of mine. The design is different but similar. I expect the same craftsman did them both. Note the delicacy of the treatment and the rare beauty of the carving."

For the first time Fancy really looked at the carving in the panel over the fireplace. What a strange man the Earl was. Imagine a lord taking an interest in architecture. She would never have believed it. It seemed that there was much more to the Earl of Morgane than appeared on the surface.

He gazed up at the ceiling. "Yes, I like this very much. Adam always had a good eye for ceilings.

Note how the shape of the ceiling is picked up in the carpet. I believe his ceilings are his most outstanding contribution to the decorative arts."

He stared upward for another long moment. "And I expect Zucchi did the paintings. And that particular way of tinting in pale blue, green, and mauve to form a soft background for the white relief, that was an Adam innovation. Old Cavendish knew enough to leave beautiful things alone—at least."

Fancy, who had been gazing up at the ceiling with something akin to awe, felt herself bristling up at this reference to her cousin. "I'll thank you not to speak unkindly of the dead."

The Earl raised a dark eyebrow. "A thousand pardons, my dear Miss Harper. I was not aware that you harbored such tender feelings for your kinsman."

There was something in the Earl's voice that seemed to carry much more meaning than his words. It was to that something than Fancy responded. "I do not have 'tender' feelings for him," she replied rather tartly. "I never knew him."

The Earl made no reply to this but he looked plainly unconvinced.

"I do not know *why* he gave me this house, but he did. And I intend to live here—for a long time," she added defiantly.

Morgane merely nodded in agreement. "I trust you will have sense enough not to ruin the place with the addition of nouveau riche embellishments."

Fancy, to whom even the idea of doing such seemed ridiculous, merely shrugged. "I have not yet decided if I shall change the decorations. I merely wanted to get nicely settled before the season began."

The Earl smiled lazily. "An admirable goal certainly and one you seem to have attained." He looked around the drawing room with interested eyes. "Yes, I like this room. I trust the rest of the house is correspondingly well done."

"I have no training in architecture," said Fancy stiffly. "But I believe it is. I, at least, find it quite a lovely house."

"So I should imagine," agreed the Earl. "It must have been something of a surprise to one of your— background." The Earl's eyes watched her intently, almost as though waiting for an angry reaction.

Fancy took a deep breath. "Yes, it was," she replied calmly. "Though Papa and Mama did not exactly reside in hovels, we assuredly never had anything half so grand. At least Mama and I didn't. Of course, when Papa was a boy he must have lived in grand places."

The Earl's eyebrow lifted again. "How so?"

Fancy blushed. "Papa was of aristocratic blood. He was a younger son and his family disowned him when he wanted to marry Mama. But he did it anyway."

Morgane's eyes glittered dangerously. "For love, I presume," he pronounced cynically.

She would not get angry, Fancy told herself. She simply would not. "Yes, for love. People do marry for that reason. Or so I believe."

Morgane shrugged well-clad shoulders. "I find myself quite doubtful on that score. Experience has taught me that love is an illusion, a something that callow moonlings are wont to believe in until they learn better—usually in quite a painful fashion."

With difficulty Fancy kept her tongue between her teeth. She could not let him know that she had been informed about his past. She did not want to cause dissension between him and Castleford. "I'm afraid I must disagree with you, milord," she replied finally. "I believe that many people marry because of a real partiality for each other."

"Perhaps," answered the Earl, with no great conviction in his tone. "And perhaps they marry for other reasons—like title and money."

"That is not something I would do," rejoined Fancy.

The Earl raised an eyebrow but made no direct comment on this. "Are you not a curious advocate for the emotion of love?" he asked.

"Why?" *What was the man getting at now?* Fancy wondered.

"You have told me more than once—in no uncertain terms"—the Earl's hand rose to his scarred cheek—"that you do not need a man. That the theater is your life."

"It is," cried Fancy. "I meant what I said."

The Earl laughed. It was not a pleasant sound, but cynical, and, Fancy thought, sad in some inexplicable fashion. "You are not being at all logical. First you tell me that love is very important and then you tell me that it is not for you."

Fancy, though she was aware of the sense of what he was saying, did not want to concede it. "I do believe in love," she said. "But not for myself. And besides"—she knew her anger was getting the better of her, but she could not help it —"what you offered me was not—love."

Instead of becoming angry, the Earl merely laughed. "*Touché.* I offered you—if I remember correctly—an establishment and jewels. And the price was not high enough."

Angrily Fancy bounced from her chair. "You are mistaken in me, milord. It was not a question of the price. I am not for sale. Not then. Not now. Not ever."

The Earl raised a quizzical eyebrow. "Come, come, my dear girl. Are you going to lose your temper when we have been dealing so famously with each other these many minutes?"

For several seconds Fancy fought with an intense desire to throw something at this irritating, top-lofty creature. But a little reflection soon reminded her that if she threw something at the Earl, it would be *her* something. And she undoubtedly would be the loser. She would also give him another opportunity to laugh at her.

83

With a deep sigh she settled back into her chair. She would not let him goad her into a temper tantrum. It was a very good thing that she had made this resolve, for the Earl's next statement made her grip the arms of her chair until her knuckles turned white.

"Very good," said he. "Quite commendable. You are learning to control that vicious temper of yours. After all, having red hair is really no excuse for behaving abominably."

Morgane seemed to be waiting for her explosion. Fancy unclenched her fingers and folded them in her lap before she replied. "My temper is no more vicious than yours," she said evenly. "And I do not throw things."

Morgane laughed. "Perhaps not, but you *want* to."

To this Fancy could make no adequate reply. She would not deny the truth, but neither did she want to admit to it. She decided to remain silent.

The Earl cast his glance once more at the ceiling. "Yes," he nodded. "Even the incongruity of mixing winged sphinxes, dolphins, and griffins with the serrated leaves of the acanthus, the flowers of the honeysuckle, and the long pendant catkins of the Garraya Elliptica cannot mar its beauty."

He returned his gaze to the fireplace. "If I were you, I should let no one touch that beauty either. That's a rare white marble he used and the stucco ornaments under the mantel are quite well done."

Fancy found herself obediently examining the

items he had pointed out. Even in her anger she could discern fresh beauties, beauties she had been too busy previously to notice.

The Earl rose from his chair and began to make a leisurely tour of the room, pausing now and then before one of the wall panels that held decorative paintings. In spite of herself, Fancy found that she was twisting in her chair to watch his progress.

He completed the tour of the room and paused before the panel to the left of the fireplace. Then he nodded. "Yes, this whole room is a specimen of Adam's best work." He chuckled. "The man was extremely clever. He couldn't bear to have his beautiful rooms destroyed by the hanging of a faulty picture. And so, many times he had the paintings themselves designed right into the room. In this way the owner was prevented from destroying the unity of Adam's creation."

Fancy, eyeing the paintings, each in its own panel, was forced to acknowledge the truth of the Earl's words.

"I believe," said Morgane thoughtfully, "that I prefer the romantic landscapes that grace my drawing room to these classical groups in chiaroscuro. Studies in light and shade, with no regard to color, are interesting, but not as restful to the tired mind as a good landscape."

"Of course, I have not seen your landscapes, milord," replied Fancy. "But I find this drawing room quite adequate for my needs."

The Earl chuckled again. "I expect you do. I

85

collect that great hordes of visitors are not descending upon you."

Fancy stifled a sharp retort. Castleford had obviously not wanted his visit to be known to his friend and she would respect his confidence. She summoned a smile. "You are quite right, milord. I receive few visitors. But, as I told you before, I do not set up to be a lady. This is a nice house—" The Earl's eyebrow rose again but he said nothing. "This is a very nice house," continued Fancy. "Perhaps a little grand for the likes of me. But I intend to stay here and enjoy it. Especially now that I have been apprised of so many of its beauties," she added, with a mischievous smile. "And, since I do not need my neighbors in order to enjoy myself, I really need not care about their feelings in the matter."

A glint of amusement flickered in the Earl's cool eyes. "A selfish sentiment, very admirable for a lady," he replied. "You are perhaps further on your way to that estate than you suppose."

Fancy refused to be riled. "That doesn't signify. I have no wish to be a lady. I find ladies intolerably stuffy and dull. And as for lords—" Fancy shrugged daintily.

The Earl laughed. "Your estimation of our character is perhaps more accurate than we would like to admit. A position in the *haut ton* is perhaps not the enviable thing many people feel it to be."

This disclosure on the part of the Earl took Fancy somewhat by surprise. She would never have expected the haughty Morgane to say a thing against riches and position, but then the Earl appeared to have many divergent aspects to him.

"I would not know about that," said Fancy with a little grimace. "However, I do know that I am a working woman and this time after dinner is a time in which I study my lines so—"

"So you would like me to leave," said the Earl.

"That would be most helpful," replied Fancy. To her dismay, however, the Earl reseated himself and stretched his long legs with a sigh of contentment.

"I am sorry to keep you from your work," said he in a tone that evidenced no sorrow whatsoever, "but I believe we have some unfinished business to discuss."

Fancy felt herself coloring up. "I have already told you—" she began.

But the Earl interrupted her. "I do not mean *that* business. Though I do not yet consider the matter closed. I mean the business of that creature you dignify with the name of dog."

"Oh!" Fancy fought to regain her composure. What an insufferable creature he was. Always so haughty and disdainful. And so often right!

"I have already said that I will pay for any damages that Hercules has caused."

The Earl chuckled. "An admirable recovery. You have great stage presence. It would serve you well with an audience."

Fancy chose to ignore this. "Did my dog do any damage to your door?" she asked.

The Earl shook his head. "To the best of my knowledge," said he, "my door is intact. The damage to my nerves, however—"

Fancy suddenly found herself breaking into laughter.

Morgane eyed her quizzically.

"I am sorry, milord, but you do not play the part at all well. Your nerves, if you have *any*, are undoubtedly made of iron. That anything should distress you seems to me quite unimaginable. You simply cannot play the nervous beau."

Since the Earl did not seem to take any of this amiss, Fancy continued. "You might make a rather good hero," she mused, "but I believe that it is in the part of the villian that you would undoubtedly excel." She rose, hoping that the Earl would do likewise.

Fancy shifted nervously backward as the Earl rose suddenly to his feet and moved swiftly toward her. His eyes, when they met hers, were still cool and gray, but the scar had taken on that peculiar hue that marked his anger. "If I were you," he said evenly, stopping less than a foot from her and holding her eyes with his, "I should be more careful what I said to a man of such vicious temper and villainous character as you believe me to have."

Fancy, her eyes locked in the grip of those gray ones, found herself trembling. He was so close and so powerful. And the drawing room door was closed. If he reached out for her, if he swept her into his arms, would she have time to cry out before his savage brutal kiss claimed her lips?

She tried to tear her eyes away from his, but she was unable to do so. For long moments he kept her captive with that overpowering gaze. And then a cynical smile curved his thin lips. "No need to play the startled maiden," he remarked sarcastically. "This evening I am not in the mood to play the villian. So you are safe—for the moment."

Fancy dropped her eyes in confusion. She had been foolish to antagonize the man. But she would not apologize.

As she raised her eyes, he spoke again. "I must thank you for a very pleasant visit. Perhaps at some future date I shall be invited to return for a tour of the whole house. In the meantime I trust you will keep that door-wrecker under lock and key."

With that the Earl turned away and, bowing ironically, let himself out of the drawing room. Fancy could hear him in the hall, urbanely bidding Henry farewell. For long minutes after she heard the heavy door close behind him she stood unseeing, staring at one of the chiaroscuro paintings. Then she shook her head and spoke sharply to herself. The Earl of Morgane was no concern of hers. No concern at all. She would just keep Hercules at home and she would not see the Earl again.

The thought sounded good, but as she picked

up her script and began to review her lines, Fancy was aware of a feeling strangely like disappointment. It could not *be* disappointment, she told herself sternly. For she would not be at all unhappy should the Earl of Morgane never again bring his handsome self into her presence. And with that she again resumed her practice, determined to keep all further thoughts of his darkly handsome features from her mind.

Chapter Six

The next several days found Fancy busy practicing her lines. *The School of Reform* was an addition to her repertoire and since she was also going to play Mrs. Kitely in *Every Man in His Humour* and had small parts in other plays, she had a great deal to do, reviewing her lines and refreshing her characters. Morning rehearsals, afternoon rehearsals, costume fittings, these things took time too.

She did not go to the theater to see Mr. Shuffleton in *John Bull* on Friday, since she had no part in that play. Nor did she attend on Saturday, Henry and Ethel having prevailed upon her to stay home. As Ethel had so succinctly put it, "Ain't no use asking for trouble. They don't need you for nothing down there. No use in going."

So Fancy had remained at home, immuring herself in her lines. Knowing that soon she would be facing an audience again, she was able to handle her loneliness. Living in the great house, actually very much alone in spite of all the people surrounding her, did not suit Fancy's temperament. From childhood she had known the hustle and bustle of stage life, always surrounded by busy, active people, always a part of something exciting.

Here in this great house she felt very alone. Even Henry and Ethel, who had always been her friends, now seemed distant. Sometimes Fancy found herself wishing for the jolly old days in Bath when she had been just another struggling young player.

It was in this not so joyful mood that Cooke found her when Henry ushered him into the little sitting room that she most often used. "Uncle George!" Fancy rushed to throw herself into his arms. He held her briefly and then stepped back. Fancy breathed a sigh of relief: he did not smell of gin. That day he had not been drinking. "Come and sit down, Uncle George. Or would you like to see the house first?"

Cooke shrugged his shoulders. "A house is a house, though this appears to be a mighty fine one."

Fancy sighed. "It is. Mighty fine and mighty lonely."

"Then why do you stay here?" Cooke's eyes regarded her shrewdly.

Fancy shrugged. "It's a very nice house, Uncle

George. And I'll get used to it. Besides, in a few days I'll be acting almost every night. That's what I need. To be on—"

The look on Cooke's face stopped her. "Uncle George! What is it? What's wrong?"

Cooke settled heavily into a chair. "They've closed the theater. Last night. You won't be acting for a while, I'm afraid."

Fancy sank into a nearby chair. "How long?"

Cooke shook his head. "We don't know. Kemble felt it best to close. He canceled Catalani and the house will be closed till the accounts have been examined by competent gentlemen. There's no sense in performing for a crowd like that. The rioting's been bad every night. Though not quite as bad as Wednesday when—" He paused and looked embarrassed.

Fancy hurried to reassure him. "Uncle George, please, you mustn't feel bad. I wasn't hurt at all. And it wasn't your fault. Really, it wasn't."

Cooke shook his head, but did not reply to this.

"Why do they have to riot like this?" asked Fancy.

Cooke shrugged. "Obviously the theatergoers are not the enlightened and liberal public that Kemble thought they would be on opening night." He shook his head. "No one can continue acting under all that tension. The company was all nerves."

Fancy nodded. "I know. It was very bad."

Cooke sighed. "That's one of the worst audiences I've ever seen. And I've seen plenty in my time."

93

"So what did Mr. Kemble do?"

"He addressed the audience, or tried to. He told them that the proprietors were most anxious to do everything in their power to meet the public inclination and restore the public peace. Personally, I don't think anything's going to work but a reduction in prices. So he said the proprietors were willing to have a committee of respectable gentlemen appointed to inspect things, including the profits. And to say whether or not the advance was warranted. And until the examination is over the theater will be shut down."

Fancy sighed. "I hope it doesn't take too long. I need to be acting."

Cooke eyed her solemnly. "You're looking a little peaked, Fancy, m'girl. I don't think this place agrees with you."

Fancy laughed. "I suppose I could sell it and move elsewhere, but that would be running."

"Running? I don't understand."

Fancy managed a little smile. "My neighbors are not exactly friendly. The Earl of Morgane, especially, has suggested that I will not be happy in this neighborhood."

Cooke whistled. "Morgane! Fancy, m'girl, you'd better watch your step with that one. I thought he was being sort of high-handed with you the other night. So you knew him before?"

Fancy nodded. She did not think it wise to give Uncle George a complete picture of her meetings with the conceited Earl. "He is a most exasperating man," she said, her green eyes flashing. "But I do not intend to let him run *my* life."

Cooke smiled wearily. "The Earl is used to running things, m'girl. You'd better get that through your noggin immediately. If you mix with him—" Cooke shook his head. "The Earl's never been known to knuckle under. Why, he boxed Gentleman Jackson when the Earl was just a stripling. He wouldn't give up, kept struggling to his feet. The man's no quitter, Fancy, m'girl. Best think carefully before you come to cuffs with him. He can be an ugly customer."

Fancy tossed her copper curls defiantly. "I don't care about that the least bit," she averred. "No man is going to chase me out of this house. I can guarantee it."

Cooke laughed. "Well, well, child, don't get that temper up at me. This is old Uncle George, remember?"

Fancy laughed. "I have made great gains in controlling my temper lately," she said. "Goodness knows I have had enough practice at it. But come, let me give you a tour of the house."

Sometime later Cooke descended the staircase, shaking his head. "You've no business in a place like this. It must cost a fortune to run."

"It does, Uncle George, but that doesn't signify. The Marquis left me plenty. He must have been a kind old gentleman."

At this Cooke burst into a great fit of laughter.

"Don't be such an innocent, Fancy, m'girl. Cavendish was very active in the petticoat line. Just as much after the ladies in muslin as your friend the Earl."

Fancy bridled. "He is *not* my friend. And I never even saw the Marquis. Besides, he was an *old* man."

Cooke chuckled dryly. "For a girl your age you've a lot to learn. A man's years have nothing to do with his desire for a pretty young dasher."

Fancy flushed. "Uncle George, you are embarrassing me."

"Best to know the way the world is," observed Cooke wisely. "That way it can't take you by surprise. Speaking of which, I've some friends awaiting my arrival. I had a hankering to see your great house so I told Kemble I'd bring you the word. You're to keep learning your lines, he says. For he expects to reopen as soon as the committee makes its report."

Fancy nodded. She very much wanted to keep Uncle George from the low tavern where she suspected his friends were awaiting him with bumpers of blue ruin, but she knew that no words of hers would deter him. And so she simply said, "Take care of yourself now, Uncle George. And come back to see me."

Cooke's smile was warm, but he shook his head. "This is too much house for the likes of me. I can't be comfortable in it. But I'll see you when we reopen."

As Fancy watched him make his way to the street, she sighed heavily. Uncle George was really a nice person—except when he was in his altitudes —and he was there much too often.

She turned away with another sigh. Now she would have to stay cooped up in this big old house for how many days longer. It just wasn't fair.

Making her way toward the sitting room, Fancy rubbed at her temple absently. Life was all a muddle these days. When she'd first come to London, it had been with high spirits. There she was—with a great house and a season at Covent Garden. What more could she ask for?

But everything had suddenly gone sour. Those stupid rioters had ruined the theater and the dark man next door had spoiled her joy in this house.

Suddenly Fancy straightened her slumping shoulders. She would not allow herself to be overcome by despair. The theater would open again eventually. The committee must come to some conclusion, and then she would be back on the stage.

And she would not let the Earl browbeat her into obedience. Earls had no say over her life, she told herself defiantly. None at all.

She turned back from the sitting-room door. Enough of scripts for one day. She needed a breath of fresh air. "Henry, have you had Hercules fitted with a new collar?"

"Yes, miss."

"Good, then fetch his leash while I go for my bonnet. I want to take a walk."

"Miss Fancy—"

But Fancy was already running lightly up the stairs to fetch her new straw bonnet. As she stood before the cheval glass and tied the wide blue ribbons in a big bow under her chin, she couldn't help smiling. The bonnet was huge and the blue daisies on it seemed to nod at her. It was really a rather extreme bonnet, though entirely fashionable, but in her present intransigent mood it was just what she wanted. She scooped up a cream-colored cashmere shawl and hurried down the stairs.

"Miss Fancy, the weather's not so good. It looks like it might rain."

Fancy nodded, her green eyes gleaming with mischief. "Then I shall get wet. But in the meantime we shall have had our walk. You'll like that, won't you, Hercules?"

The great dog thumped the floor loudly with his tail and eyed the door with obvious longing, his huge pink tongue lolling from his mouth.

Fancy pulled on a pair of York tan gloves and extended a hand for the leash. "Well, Hercules, let us go."

Henry, his lips set in disapproval, opened the door. As she descended the steps and set off in the opposite direction from the Earl's house, Fancy carefully kept her eyes averted. She had no wish to give any thought at all to her horrible neighbor.

Twice around the square Fancy proceeded at a leisurely pace, taking a great interest in her surroundings. Several times gentlemen tipped their hats or nodded. They were obviously inhabitants of the neighborhood and she returned their greetings with a modest smile.

Inevitably as they passed the iron railing and the steps leading up to the Earl's great mahogany door, Hercules would begin tugging on his leash. Fancy found it difficult to account for the dog's actions. But she would set her teeth and pass resolutely on, never deigning by as much as a single glance to recognize the existence of the Earl's abode.

For all the proud set of her head and the resolute way she forced Hercules to follow her, she was intensely aware that behind the white curtained windows of the great house a pair of cool gray eyes might be following her every motion.

They were making their third round when the clatter of approaching hooves caused Fancy to turn startled eyes to the street. She turned them away again as soon as they sighted the occupant of the carriage, but not before they had been met by a pair of cool gray ones.

As the barouche clattered past and stopped immediately in front of his door, the Earl handed the reins to his groom and jumped lightly down. For a moment Fancy considered reversing directions and retracing her steps around the square. But she rejected such a cowardly thought. She would never let the top-lofty Earl believe that she was afraid to face him. No, indeed.

And so she continued her even pace and the Earl, having given directions to his groom, turned to watch her approach. The color bloomed in Fancy's cheeks, but she refused to lower her gaze or slow her step. She had as much right on this street as anyone.

Hercules, now having gotten a good look at the Earl, made a sudden lunge that tore the leash from Fancy's fingers. Then he raced down the pavement and launched himself at the Earl. Fancy, hurrying after him, uttered a cry of dismay and involuntarily closed her eyes. When she opened them, Hercules was sitting calmly on the pavement, his great tail threatening it with destruction and the Earl was calmly regarding her.

Fancy, who had expected to see the Earl measuring his length on the pavement or, at the very least, with his well-cut coat of blue superfine and his buckskin breeches liberally coated with dirt, could not suppress a cry of surprise.

"Good day, Miss Harper," said the Earl coolly. "I trust your cry of dismay is not due to the failure of your dog to lay me low."

"Of course not. Must you be so nasty?" snapped Fancy and then wished she had curbed her tongue. For certainly that flicker of amusement in the Earl's eyes was caused by her evidence of temper. His next words proved it.

"Tch, tch, you are very touchy today."

100

"The times are trying," said Fancy stiffly. "Covent Garden has been closed and I do not know when it will open again."

The Earl shrugged. "Admirable as the theater may be there *are* other things in life."

"Not for me," replied Fancy testily.

"That is because you refuse to look around you. For instance, you might spend some night training this brute here to more gentlemanly behavior."

"He is trained," said Fancy, and then, realizing she had said the wrong thing, flushed again.

The Earl chuckled, an unpleasant sound. "I am well aware of his disreputable tricks." He shook his head. "That so much beauty should be wasted."

Fancy bristled. "Hercules's tricks are not disreputable. Rather it is the lords who occasion their use that should bear that title. And my beauty, as you call it, is mine. Many men enjoy it from afar and it gives them pleasure. It is *not* wasted."

"Ah," said the Earl, his eyes fastening on hers. "Does it give *you* pleasure?"

"Of course it does!"

Morgane shook his head. "You are a strange one, Miss Fancy Harper. You pick a calling that immediately marks you for sale and then you refuse to sell."

"You are insulting me, milord," replied Fancy haughtily. "There have been great actresses who were also virtuous."

Morgane laughed. "Then they obviously kept that virtue well hidden for it was of no help to

101

them in their careers—except perhaps for the first sale."

Fancy felt her gloved fingers curling into fists. "You are a miserable human being," said she from between clenched teeth. "The aristocracy of this country certainly has fallen into ill repute."

The Earl's lips tightened into a thin line. Then he stooped and retrieved Hercules's leash. He offered it to her with a sardonic smile. "May I suggest that you take this faithful beast home before we stoop to trading insults on our parentage like a couple of irate fishwives?"

Fancy took the proffered leash. "You are quite right, milord, I find that conversation with you quickly degenerates into insult."

With a sharp tug at the leash she marched past the Earl. "Don't scold him too much," said that amazing man just as they passed him. "He really cannot help it if he prefers the company of quality."

His mocking laughter followed her as she proceeded down the street and up the steps to her own door. But Fancy dared not look back. If she saw him now, with that terrible haughty smile and those cool gray eyes, she knew she would scream. Her very fingers inside her glove itched to make contact with that assured smirking face.

Someday, she thought as she banged the knocker sharply, someday she would give the Earl such a set down that he would never recover from it.

As the door opened she thrust the leash into

Henry's hand and said crisply, "See that this vile dog is taught some manners and see to it immediately."

"Yes, Miss Fancy. Right away." And Henry, who had witnessed the whole of his young mistress's encounter with the Earl, wisely refrained from asking any questions. When Fancy's eyes glittered with anger like that, the best thing, he had learned, was to leave her to work it out herself. His lips curved in an enigmatic smile as she mounted the stairs. Whatever was between Miss Fancy Harper and the Earl of Morgane was going to take a great deal of working out. That much, at least, seemed certain.

Chapter Seven

The days passed slowly for Fancy, very slowly. She studied her lines and, when she could stand that no longer, she wandered around through the rooms of the great house that had become, by such a quirk of fate, her home, and studied it. This pursuit served to alleviate some of her boredom, for the house was undoubtedly a piece of beautiful workmanship. Every trip through it uncovered further beauties to Fancy's now discerning eye.

And, in the latter part of the day, when the weather was good, she took Hercules for several rounds of the square. Though every day she left her door internally braced for a confrontation with the Earl, the occasion never arose, that gentleman either avoiding her or, what seemed more likely to Fancy, having dismissed her from his consciousness as not worthy of his bother.

During this time a close watch was kept on Hercules and despite his earnest endeavors in that direction he did not manage to escape through the front door.

And finally the waited-for news came from Covent Garden. The theater would open again on October 4 with *The Beggar's Opera*. Fancy, greatly relieved, immediately made plans to attend every performance in spite of Ethel's sour observation that she was behaving like a ninny.

Several weeks passed and Fancy was beginning to feel less intimidated, especially since the proprietors, after discovering that the report of the committee in their favor did nothing to convince the rioters of the rightness of their cause, hired some well-known pugilists led by the great Mendoza—to keep order in the crowd. They did not succeed very well at this task, but Fancy did feel that if she should again be pulled from the stage the pugilists would rescue her. She would not be left to the mercy of the mob or that of Morgane.

In spite of all her endeavors to the contrary, Fancy could not drive the image of the Earl's saturnine face from her mind. At the oddest moments it would reappear there and she would feel those cool gray eyes raking her body or see those thin lips curling sardonically.

Wherever the Earl had been during those days

that Covent Garden was closed, he was now very much in town. Every night from her vantage point in the wings, she saw him enter his box, the big blond Castleford beside him. It was easy enough, too, to see that the eyes of many women followed that handsome pair. That they were really prime articles, Fancy was forced to admit. The Earl's dark sinister looks were admirably set off by the open heartiness of Castleford.

Ladies, clad in satin and silk, wearing diamonds of the first water, seemed inordinately pleased at the merest nod from the Earl. And those charmers who were so favored by the scrutiny of his raised quizzing glass seemed to think themselves the recipients of a great honor.

Fancy, observing all this, raised a disdainful eyebrow. How could those women be such fools? Admittedly the Earl was a very attractive man. But did they care nothing for character, those gay butterflies who colored under his gaze or those even more amazing ones who calmly scrutinized him first?

Fancy could not understand such creatures. The Earl must have been right about one thing, though, she thought. Those beauties must lead exceedingly dull lives.

And so more nights passed and it was Saturday, time for Egerton's London debut as Lord Avondale in *The School of Reform*. Fancy hoped that the crowd would be in one of its less violent moods. Sometimes, though rarely, the rioters did not appear. But most of the time they were still there, screaming, shouting, whistling, waving banners, doing all they could to disrupt the proceedings on the stage.

The finding of the reputable committee—that the proposed prices would yield only a profit of 3½ percent rather than the 6½ percent from the old Covent Garden before the fire—seemed to have had no effect on them. The mob had no regard for logic or facts. Their minds seemed intent on the old price figure and nothing else would satisfy them.

They staged races up and down the pit benches while the play was in progress. Here and there she could see men with huge false noses and others dressed like women who swaggered and straddled about the house.

That evening there had been some disturbance at the entrance of the Duke of York during the second act. Though Parliament had exonerated him, many people were not yet sure that he was innocent in the affair of Mary Anne Clarke.

Fancy recalled Henry and Ethel discussing the scandal while they were still in Bath. "He did right to get rid of her," Henry said. "A man in his position has got to be careful. Why, he had to resign as Commander in Chief of the army and all on account of her."

"I ain't holding none for ladies of that kind," Ethel averred with a glance at Fancy. "Me being a decent married woman and all. But I says the

Duke should of known better. A woman of that stripe."

"She has courage besides her beauty," said Henry. "And they say she really stood up to the House."

Ethel nodded. "Course she did. Them women ain't got no sense of wrong. But if what they say is true—that the Duke promised her £1,000 a month and then didn't pay—I expect she figured she had the right to sell them commissions."

Henry shook his head. "They say she kept ten horses and twenty servants, including three French chefs. She ate off plate that had belonged to the Duc de Berri—gold and silver—and she paid two guineas for each of her wineglasses."

This kind of affluence had staggered Fancy's mind in those days before the death of the Marquis had put her on St. James's Square.

"Exactly what did she do?" asked Fancy, who was usually too busy with the stage to attend much to gossip.

Ethel's mouth tightened grimly. "Some says she took money from them as wanted commissions in the army and then she whispered in the Duke's ear till he give them."

"Is she very beautiful?" asked Fancy.

"Aye," said Henry. "They say she's a great beauty. And full of wit. Though they've shut her mouth now with a pension and shipped her off to the continent to live.

"I don't know as I believe the tale of her just

adding names to the lists that she copied for the Duke and him signing them without reading them," Henry added. "But it could be true."

"It's my belief they was both in the wrong." Ethel's expression reflected her disgust with such goings on. "The Duke's got a Duchess, a kind, good-natured one, too, so I hears. Let him stay home with her."

Henry smiled and patted his wife on the shoulder. "Now, Ethel, we both know that's not the way of royalty."

Fancy, remembering all this, took her next free period to peek at the Duke from the wings. His round face seemed affable and somehow she was inclined to believe in his innocence. Certainly with an older brother like the Prince of Wales, whose amorous adventures had reached even her uncaring ears, he could not be expected to be a paragon of virtue. He did look like a person who would not be difficult to get along with. No touch in his features of the hauteur that marked so many lords —and one dark one in particular.

Several times during the course of the play Fancy saw York raise his quizzing glass and survey a particular female member of the cast. But she did not think anything much of it until after the performance when she was busy removing make-up in the dressing room. It was then that the girl burst in to say excitedly, "Did you see the Duke of York?"

Fancy nodded, absently wiping the greasepaint from her cheeks.

"They say he's looking for a new dasher. Someone to replace Mary Anne Clarke."

Fancy merely shrugged. The vagaries of royalty were of little concern to her.

"How can you act that way? If he was looking like that at *me*—"

Fancy stiffened suddenly. "Do you mean that the Duke of York was ogling *me?*"

"Of course. Didn't you notice? Are you ever the lucky one!"

Fancy had no reply to this. Obviously this girl would never believe her if she insisted that this was *not* lucky. Would things in her life never return to their even tenor? The last thing she wanted was the amorous attentions of the Duke of York.

She scrubbed furiously at her face. It was one thing to scoff at Morgane, to laugh at Castleford, but how was she to refuse a member of the royal family?

When the after-piece was over and performers adjourned to the greenroom to receive the plaudits of their admirers, if any such existed in the audience, Fancy still had no answer to this question, but on one thing she was still determined. The stage was her love and no man, royal or not, was going to change that. He would simply have to accept the fact that she was not for sale. No man would ever own her.

Stepping through the door into the greenroom,

she eyed the throng nervously, and then, not seeing the somewhat portly figure of the Duke, she breathed a sigh of relief and moved to join Egerton, who was animatedly talking to a young woman, a minor member of the company.

"I have never seen such a crowd," said he. "And I have faced some bad ones. Imagine, tonight they had a flaming banner in the street."

The girl, Annie, shivered in horror. "We shall all be killed one of these nights," she whimpered.

"Nonsense," insisted Fancy. "They do not mean to hurt us."

Annie shook her head. "I should have died, just died, if they'd pulled me off the stage and tumbled me about."

Fancy regarded the plaintive young woman with a skeptical eye. According to current gossip, Annie had been "tumbled about" by more than one gentleman in her brief time as an actress. But even Fancy could see that in being tumbled it made a difference who was *doing* the tumbling. So she merely shrugged. "I am certainly not any worse for the experience, as you can plainly see."

Annie smiled smugly. "I guess not. Not when the Earl of Morgane himself rescues you." She heaved a plaintive sigh. "Such an out-and-outer. A prime article."

"I do not find the Earl's regard for me a happy circumstance," replied Fancy disdainfully.

Annie rolled her eyes. "My, ain't we being high and mighty, though?" She tossed her cap of blond curls. "I'll tell you one thing, the Earl can have a regard for me any day in the week and twice on Sundays!"

"I'm afraid I shall have to decline that honor, my affections being otherwise engaged." Both women whirled to find themselves facing the Earl and his friend Castleford.

"Oh, milord," simpered Annie, batting her eyes in a way that made Fancy long to smack her, "I hope you ain't offended."

The Earl did not smile. "Since I presume no offense was meant, none has been taken." He shifted his attention to Fancy in such a manner that Annie had little choice but to consider herself dismissed.

"Good evening, Miss Harper," said the Earl urbanely, raising her hand swiftly to his lips. They barely brushed the backs of her fingers, and Fancy was startled by the realization that his lips were warm! That must account for the strange feeling that assailed her at their touch.

"I do not find the evening particularly good," returned Fancy curtly, to the obvious surprise of Egerton who was looking from one to the other in an effort to discover what the situation was.

Castleford apparently decided to pour oil on troubled waters. "May I congratulate you on your performance, Miss Harper?"

Fancy could not help smiling at Castleford's rather clumsy attempt to make peace. "Thank you,

112

milord. I believe I did tolerably well, though I doubt you heard much of what I said."

"But what I heard was lovely," said a new voice. Fancy tried not to color up as the Duke of York joined their circle and surveyed her through his quizzing glass.

"Thank you, Your Royal Highness," she managed to mumble. Then, aware of the Earl's sardonic eyes, she straightened and returned the Duke's gaze. Up close she could see that he was a fine specimen of manhood. Six feet tall, with a broad chest and muscular frame. A little gone to stoutness, perhaps, but not enough to detract from his military bearing.

Certainly his face was handsome, with a full prominent brow from under which his gray eyes beamed with benevolence. It was a face that bore the look of authority, but it was a kind face too. The army, thought Fancy, had been fortunate to have this man as commander in chief. He looked like a man who cared about his troops.

The Duke continued to beam upon her and Fancy returned his smile with a demure one of her own. There seemed little else to do. But she began to feel rather uneasy. For a certain glint in the Duke's gray eyes led her to believe that the girl in the dressing room had been right.

Certainly she had nothing against York. And if she were in the market for a protector, certainly his warm gray eyes held the promise of a more thoughtful kindness than did the cool ones of the Earl. She had better just move quietly away. She simply could not bear it, she told herself, if York made her an offer right in front of that top-lofty Earl. She would just slip back to the dressing room and no one would be the wiser.

And so, when York turned to address Egerton, she did just that. But Fancy had reckoned without the Earl. She had her hand on the knob to the dressing-room door when his hand on her shoulder stopped her.

She turned to face him. "I have something to say to you," said that irritating man, his cool gray eyes noting her expression.

Fancy, already nerved up from the tension of the evening, felt her control snap. "I have nothing to say to you," she cried, turning back to the door.

Two strong hands fastened on her shoulders and spun her around to face him. Fancy felt her heart rise in her throat at seeing that dark face so close to her own. "You *will* listen to me," said the Earl evenly.

Fancy struggled to free herself from his grip. The Earl merely smiled. "You may call for help if you choose, but when it arrives, I can assure you that your reputation will be liberally besmirched."

"What—what do you want of me?" Fancy faltered.

The Earl smiled sardonically. "I had thought by now to have made myself quite clear on that score.

I have even considered raising the price, though that goes against my principles."

"The answer is still no," cried Fancy. "I cannot be bought."

Morgane smiled; it was not a pleasant sight. "Plump in the pocket as I am, I cannot compete with York. But let me remind you that his promises are only that—promises. Certainly the case of Mistress Clarke proves that. Whereas you may ask almost any lady of the *ton* and be assured that debts of this amorous nature are always paid promptly by myself. Ergo, I am the better choice."

He smiled and leaned closer. Fancy felt her heart fluttering in her throat. If he kissed her again now, she would simply die. Yet she was powerless to loosen his grasp.

"Also," he continued, a glint of humor in his eye, "I am, as anyone can see, in better physical condition and younger than His Royal Highness. I am also quite probably more proficient in matters of this nature, having given them considerable study."

Finally, Fancy found her tongue. "Undoubtedly you have had more experience with loose women than has York. I do not see that as any cause for rejoicing. In fact, I find it reprehensible."

His grip on her arms tightened painfully, but she refused to cry out.

"You are enough to drive a man to violence," said Morgane from between clenched teeth. "I am two and thirty years old. During those years I have not resided in a fairy-tale world of princes and heroes. Instead I have lived in a very real world of needs. I have filled those needs in the best way possible. I am still endeavoring to fill them."

"You will not fill them with *me*," cried Fancy defiantly. "I am not a thing to be used. And—and if you were the last man on earth and I were starving, I would prefer death to survival in your company!"

The Earl's face blanched and his control, too, seemed gone. He shook her violently, her copper curls bouncing against her shoulders. "You are the most impossible specimen of a female that I have ever had the misfortune to encounter. You are a spoiled brat, an upstart little chit who doesn't know her place."

Fancy, her head bouncing, could not think. He was too strong for her. She could only hang helpless in his grasp.

"Morgane!" Castleford's voice rang out in horror. "My God, man, what are you doing?"

The Earl ceased shaking her. For a moment she hung weakly in his grasp. Then his hands loosened and as her rubbery legs were about to collapse under her, a pair of arms surrounded her. "There now, Miss Harper, are you all right? Morgane must have lost his senses."

For a moment Fancy leaned gratefully against the broad expanse of Castleford's waistcoat. Then she struggled upright and pulled away. "Thank you, milord."

Castleford's usually friendly face looked exceedingly stern. He watched her for a moment to see that she was able to stand and then he turned to Morgane.

"Your conduct toward Miss Harper has been reprehensible," said he. "I must insist on an apology."

Morgane remained silent, his gray eyes still glinting with anger.

"William—" Castleford's voice held a note of sadness.

Suddenly Fancy realized what was going on. Castleford was expecting Morgane to apologize to her. And if he did not—the Marquis would call him out!

"No! Stop!" Fancy moved between the men. "Milord, you must not. I am not hurt."

Castleford shook his head stubbornly. "As a gentleman I must insist that the Earl apologize to you, or—"

"No!" Fancy was filled with terror. She could not let these men—men who had been lifelong friends—fight a duel over her. Her imagination painted a terrifying picture in which they both lay dead or dying.

"Please, milord." In her distress she clung to Castleford's arm. "It was my fault. I—I provoked him. Oh, please!"

Castleford seemed torn by indecision. It was obvious he did not want to meet his friend, but he was genuinely concerned for her.

Suddenly Fancy had an inspiration. "Milord Castleford, if you call out the Earl, I shall never let you into my presence again."

Castleford seemed surprised by this statement. He considered it for a few moments and then bowed his head. Perhaps, thought Fancy, to hide his relief.

"All right, Miss Harper. I concede to your wishes. But only because of my extreme regard for you."

"Thank you, milord." Fancy looked from one man to the other. "And now, if you wish to keep my regard, give me your word that you will not quarrel over me with your friend the Earl."

Even Morgane seemed surprised at this request. For a long moment Castleford's blue eyes gazed into Fancy's. He seemed to approve of what he saw there. When he spoke his voice thickened with emotion. "You have my word, Miss Harper. I shall pick no quarrel with my friend over you."

"And you?" Fancy forced herself to turn and meet the eyes of the Earl. His face was blank, his eyes devoid of all expression, but she believed that his voice, too, held a hint of emotion. "I have no wish to pick a quarrel with the friend of my boyhood and youth. Nor should I have let him provoke me into such." The Earl's eyes seemed to be searching hers, seeking something. But what it could be Fancy was at a loss to know. For all that she could read on the Earl's face, he still regarded her as a selfish brat. But Fancy could not bother about that.

She put a trembling hand to her head. "I'm afraid I must ask you gentlemen to excuse me now. I have had a rather trying day and I find that I am quite exhausted. All I wish at this moment is to find my carriage and go home."

Castleford's face wrinkled in concern. "Of course, Miss Harper. Shall I call your carriage for you?"

Fancy inclined her head gratefully. "That would be most kind of you, milord. Henry should be outside with the carriage."

"I'll go now, Miss Harper." Castleford's eyes turned to the Earl. "Will you go with me, Morgane?"

"Of course." Before he moved away the Earl's eyes met hers briefly. "I still think, Miss Harper, that you would be wise to leave the theater. It is not the place for a woman of your sensibility."

Before Fancy could think of a reply to this rather strange statement, delivered as it was in an extremely friendly tone, the Earl had followed his friend down the hall and out of sight.

Now, thought Fancy, with a sigh of exasperation, *what on earth did the man mean by that?* What kind of sensibility did he think she had? Was his statement a compliment or an insult?

She was still standing there, trying to puzzle it out, when Henry came to lead her to the carriage.

Chapter Eight

When Fancy woke on Sunday, it was with memories of the nightmares that had haunted her sleep. Sometimes both Morgane and Castleford had been lying dead, their bodies covered with bloody wounds. Other times one or the other was standing, a smoking pistol in his hand, and an expression of absolute horror on his face, over the body of his dead friend. From these terrifying visions, Fancy woke sobbing, to stare into the darkness and offer thankful prayers that she had been able to avert such a tragedy.

Whatever had possessed the Marquis to do such a thing? How vividly she could recall him saying that since that day he had stood as the young Earl's second he had never wished to duel. And yet he had been about to challenge his best friend—and over a little thing like Morgane shaking her.

Fancy suddenly clutched at the covers. My God! Castleford had conceived a real partiality for her. So strong that he was willing to fight for her.

Fancy heaved a great sigh. What strange creatures men were. She had no feelings of partiality for either man and she certainly had no wish to have them fighting over her. Why couldn't they just go about whatever it was that lords did with themselves and leave her alone?

She rose from the old bed, pushing aside the deep green hangings, and moved to the window that looked out into the courtyard. It was the end of October and autumn was certainly upon them. However, on this particular day the sun was shining rather brightly.

Down in the courtyard, sprawled in ungainly fashion upon the paving, Hercules was soaking up that sun. Fancy shook her head. Every time the front door opened the great dog was there, eager as a puppy to slip out to freedom—and probably, she thought with a grimace, to throw his huge bulk against the new mahogany door of the high and mighty Earl of Morgane. Well, thankfully so far the dog had not succeeded. She wanted no more coming to cuffs with the Earl, thank you.

With a small sigh she turned to the closet. It was time to dress for another long day at home. Critically she eyed the gowns hanging there, gowns stitched up by the modish dressmaker that Ethel had uncovered. Finally she reached for one of pale green bombazine. Its square-cut neck was trimmed with deep green velvet braid. Another strand of braid ran around under the high-waisted gathered bodice. The sleeves—long and fitted, except where they issued from the little puffs at her shoulders—were also trimmed with the velvet braid. It was a lovely dress and it became her quite well. Even in her disgruntled state Fancy could see that.

She smoothed at the skirt. She had absolutely refused to have a dresser added to her establishment. Footmen, coachman, even French chefs, but no female was needed to help Fancy Harper get into her clothes or take care of her hair. No indeed.

With another sigh she picked up the brush and attacked the tangled mass of copper curls that fell to her shoulders. They were just the color that Fancy remembered her mama's to have been. She sighed yet again. If Mama and Papa had lived, would her life have been more orderly and calm? There was no way of knowing. She turned from the cheval glass and made her way downstairs to breakfast.

The day was a long one for Fancy, especially since she had risen early—long before her fashionable neighbors, she was sure.

She had studied her lines till she was sick to death of them. She had spent some time admiring the paintings and carvings that the house had been so liberally decorated with. Finally she settled with the book about Robert Adam and his architectural innovations that Henry had just lately found for her at some bookseller's.

Let that arrogant Earl come back again and she would be ready for him! More than ready. She could discourse on the new shapes of rooms Adam had introduced, on his use of stucco for exteriors, on the way he incorporated wrought-iron balconies into the overall design of his creations, and far more.

What had begun for Fancy as a way to pass a restless hour became an absorbing task. Book in hand, she wandered from room to room, marveling in each fresh glory. With infinite care she traced each of his influences through a given room.

She was thus involved in studying the front hall, much to the curiosity of several idle footmen there, when the sound of the knocker startled her.

She turned as Henry opened the door to admit Lord Castleford. The Marquis was glowing with good health. His cheerful ruddy face beamed at her as he advanced with hands outstretched. "Miss Harper, I have come to call."

"So I see," replied Fancy, more than a little amused at the Marquis's assumed tone of heartiness. Finding her hands already occupied by the book, Castleford seemed at a loss, but he recovered rather quickly.

"The sun is shining brightly. It seems a shame to be cooped up. Get your bonnet and take a turn with me in Hyde Park."

"Oh, I can't go there."

Castleford seemed amazed. "Not go to Hyde Park? And on a Sunday. Why, all the world will be there."

Fancy was sorely tempted. She hated being cooped up and she was longing for some fresh air and sunshine. "Your friend—I do not want to come between you."

Castleford smiled cheerfully. "He has given me carte blanche. He has conceded the field to me." The Marquis seemed extremely pleased at this prospect.

Fancy managed a smile. "I fear you did not hear me the other day. I do not want a husband—or a protector. I sincerely mean that."

Castleford shook his great blond head. "That's all right, Miss Harper. Thinking that way you're not likely to go off with some other man. And as long as you don't—why, I've still got a chance."

Fancy could only shake her head at this great optimism.

"Please," begged Castleford. "I promise to be good. It's deuced lonely driving in the park by myself."

Suddenly Fancy giggled. "I should like a ride in the park, milord. But I must warn you—I have in mind to wear my newest bonnet, a great straw affair that ties with white ribbons and is adorned with pink flowers."

The Marquis smiled amiably. "I should be delighted to attend you no matter what your choice of bonnet. Your beauty makes anything you wear seem quite lovely."

This was said so easily that Fancy was quite sure that the Marquis had made use of it on more than one occasion. Apparently he was not exactly a novice in the petticoat line. And certainly with his tall good looks and affable nature Castleford would make any young lady a dashing admirer.

Fancy contented herself with a demure thank you and raced, not so demurely, up the stairs, to find the aforementioned bonnet.

When she descended, a few minutes later, the bonnet was fastened securely over her copper curls, framing a face in which green eyes danced mischievously.

"Henry, I believe I shall take my cashmere shawl—the white one with the green border."

"Yes, Miss Fancy." It was impossible to tell, from his impassive face, what Henry's thoughts were, but Fancy thought she detected a gleam of approval in his eyes. She pulled on her stone-colored gloves and turned to the Marquis.

"I am ready for my first ride in Hyde Park," said she gaily.

"And it shall be a fine one. I promise you that," said Castleford heartily. "I shall be the envy of all the bucks when I arrive with such a beauty in my barouche."

Fancy was momentarily taken aback by this comment and her feelings must have been reflected in her face. Castleford laughed.

"Come, come, you are not afraid of a little ogling, are you? You who've faced a rioting crowd at Covent Garden for these many nights?"

"No-o," she replied with such hesitation that the Marquis laughed again.

"You must learn better delivery if you wish to fool anyone with a line like that," said he.

Fancy smiled cheerfully. "I will confess to you," she said in a stage whisper. "At the theater, you see, I am not myself. The audience responds to the character I am playing, not to me. But in Hyde Park I will be Fancy Harper, 'that actress'!"

Castleford roared with laughter. "Oh, that is rich. Why, all the beaux will envy me no end. They'll swarm around like bees just for the sight of you."

Fancy chuckled. The picture of herself surrounded by elegant beaux was a pleasant one. She knew from experience how enjoyable such admiration could be.

"But will they not be surprised to find you accompanied by an actress?"

"Who? Me? What else would they expe—" Castleford seemed to suddenly recollect himself. "That is, no, they won't." He grinned rather sheepishly.

"It won't matter where you come from—not a looker like you."

Fancy suppressed a giggle and took the arm that he offered her. "I shall be home later," she said to Henry, and then with great dignity she allowed the Marquis to lead her to his carriage and hand her up.

The sun was warm and bright and Fancy felt very happy—carefree and joyful in a childish way. She basked in the warmth of the sun. "My, but it's a lovely day for a ride."

"Indeed, it is. It's a shame to keep such beauty under wraps. You were meant to grace the world."

Fancy smiled to herself. Castleford had quite a collection of compliments for the ladies. And they were all so nicely vague that they were universally applicable. There was an art, she was beginning to see, to this business of being a man about town. A certain mode of dress was required—not too elegant and not too ordinary; a certain style of conversation was designed to impress the lady without really implicating the gentleman; and a certain charm and *éclat* were necessary to carry the whole thing off.

For a moment Fancy was puzzled. How was it that the Earl had acquired so many various ladybirds? It must be that the irascibility that he evidenced in her presence was not his usual manner with the ladies.

As the carriage moved briskly along the London

streets, Fancy fell to wondering what the Earl was like when he was intent on charming a bit of muslin. Certainly he did not let that hot temper of his loose on them!

She was disturbed in this reverie by Castleford saying, "Ah, Hyde Park. And just in time."

Fancy raised her eyes to survey the scene before her. Here was the strangest thing. The park was quite large. In the far distance cows and deer grazed peacefully near each other; no people around at all. But close at hand it seemed that all the people in London had decided they must visit the park at once. In a sort of ring well-dressed people were promenading, apparently oblivious to the crowd around them except when they met someone they knew. In another place, along a road, horses and carriages met and passed, their drivers and passengers nodding briskly or staring each other down.

The dust that all this activity raised hung heavy in the air. "Can't we drive over there?" asked Fancy, pointing in a direction away from the scene of turmoil and confusion.

The Marquis raised a startled eyebrow. "Miss Harper, how can you say such a thing? In Hyde Park one rides where everyone else does. It is not *haut ton* to go off by oneself."

The *haut ton,* thought Fancy, though she did not voice her opinion aloud, must be a stupid sort to consent to milling round and round in such senseless fashion. It was inconceivable that anyone could enjoy swallowing all that dust. And conversation with anyone one met was rendered very difficult by the press of carriages or people before and behind. Nevertheless, since the Marquis was the one running this show, she nodded.

Castleford's driver, obviously well versed in the ways of the park, maneuvered their carriage into the line that came and went upon the road. "This is Rotten Row," observed the Marquis. He chuckled at Fancy's look of inquiry. "So called, I believe, because of the character of the road, and not of those who ride upon it."

Fancy chuckled, too. Castleford was a pleasant companion, easy to get along with, not like that arrogant irritating man who thought he could run her life. Her eyes swept up and down the road and suddenly she realized that she was looking for the Earl's dark locks among the dense throng.

How stupid, she told herself. Morgane was the last man she wanted to see—ever. But what had he meant by giving his friend carte blanche in that way? To her surprise she discovered that she was annoyed.

It was not, she hastened to assure herself, that the Earl meant anything to her, but simply that she did not like his offhand way of doing things. What right had he to give her to Castleford? It was almost as though, knowing he could have her whenever he chose, he had magnanimously given up the field to his friend. The nerve of the man!

Fancy began to bristle up. The Earl had better

not show his darkly handsome face, or she would give it another smack, she thought defiantly.

Castleford, completely oblivious to what was going on in her mind, was occupied with nodding and returning greetings. He turned to her. "You are getting a lot of attention. Just as I said."

Suddenly brought back to her present situation, Fancy hoped that she had not let her anger be reflected on her face. Certainly Castleford's friends would think it strange that he should be squiring a scowling young woman through the Park.

A tall handsome man in uniform in a passing carriage fixed his eyeglass and ogled Fancy approvingly. "Who is he?" she asked curiously.

Castleford shrugged. "That's Colonel Dan Mackinnon. A great swell. And a great man with the ladies. But hardhearted," added the Marquis. "And fickle."

"How so?" Fancy found Castleford very amusing. In the theater it had been assumed among the actresses that men, at least rich aristocratic ones, were always fickle. Yet the Marquis was talking as though most lords were men of honor in regard to affairs of the heart.

"He's a great favorite with the fair sex, but not long ago he decided to end an affair with a lady, a highborn lady. When he failed to visit her, she wrote, demanding that he return a lock of hair she had given him."

Fancy shook her head. "That was foolish."

"Indeed, it was," agreed Castleford. "For Mackinnon sent round his orderly with a large packet of locks of hair—of every color—and a message telling her to choose her own."

Fancy frowned. "She was doubly foolish to care for such a man. After hearing this I am even more certain that I do not wish to get emotionally tangled with a man."

Castleford looked crestfallen. "I thought to warn you against Mackinnon's black eyes and splendid figure, not against all men. We are not all the same."

"I am sure you are not," returned Fancy in a soothing tone. "But tell me truthfully, milord, have you not indicated to me that your desire in regard to me is rather like that of Mackinnon when he meets a new ladybird?"

The Marquis flushed. "Yes, but—but I should do well by you. Give you an establishment. Take care of you. And I should intend our liaison to be a lasting one. After all, look how long William, Duke of Clarence, has been living with Mrs. Jordan and they get along famously."

"I realize that your intentions are good," said Fancy gently. "But recollect, Lord Castleford. I *have* an establishment."

"But you do not have a friend and protector," stammered Castleford.

"No, I do not. But I have no need for one."

The Marquis shook his head dismally. "To live without love is unhealthy. I can accept that you have no partiality for me. But that you should

131

never care for anyone—that concerns me, for your sake."

Fancy smiled. "Do not upset yourself about me, milord. I have not met any man for whom I can conceive a partiality. I have not been, like most girls, raised to think of matrimony. My life is the stage. It has been so since before I was eight."

Castleford smiled. "The stage need not preclude your having an alliance. Most actresses do."

Fancy could only agree with this, but she did not like to say so. Fortunately, at that moment they passed a carriage containing a slight darkhaired woman, whose deep-fringed eyes surveyed Fancy coldly before they moved on to Castleford and warmed into a seductive smile.

Fancy fought off a shiver of dread. That woman hated other women; she could feel it in her bones.

"That was Lady Jersey," commented Castleford. "An elegant-looking woman. One of the patronesses of Almack's."

Fancy shruggged inwardly. So, that was the haughty Lady Jersey to whom the *ton* must bow. How happy she was not to be bothered by such absurdity.

"Do you go often to Almack's?" she asked. Not because she was interested in that place, but because she wished to move the conversation away from alliances.

Castleford nodded. "Yes, Jersey has me on her books. But it is actually a rather stuffy place. The refreshments are abominable. And it abounds in

132

fat dowager mamas with shy young daughters who wish to make suitable marriages." The Marquis frowned. "I suppose one might say that it is actually a marriage mart. The young heiresses, the extent of whose fortunes has been whispered about, are put on display for the selection of those men interested in an eligible connection."

"Why have you made no such connection?" asked Fancy, and then flushed as she realized that this was a personal question.

But Castleford did not seem offended. "I met no suitable young woman for whom I conceived a partiality. And so I thought it wiser to remain alone in my bachelor establishment."

Fancy chuckled. "I collect, milord, that as a man about town you are not excessively lonely."

Castleford grinned. "You are quite right, Miss Harper. My situation as a bachelor is one that many of my married friends envy. Though I suppose that someday I shall have to marry to carry on the line, I have given up hoping that I shall find an eligible connection to whom I may really give my heart. Heiresses seem, for some odd reason, to be born proportionately more ugly than most women."

Fancy could not help laughing at this, but Castleford shook his head. "It is true. I have been on the town these fourteen years and every season the crop of heiresses gets uglier. And," he added with a shy smile at her, "the actresses seem to get lovelier."

Fancy smiled. "Thank you, milord. You are very kind."

Castleford chuckled. "I am not kind. I am truthful."

The clatter of a carriage coming in the other direction prevented Fancy from replying. A very young man in an immense greatcoat with innumerable pockets came tooling down alongside the road. As he passed them he uttered an oath and spit a great distance through his front teeth.

Fancy stared in surprise and then turned to Castleford. "Do they allow coachmen to drive here?"

The Marquis laughed. "That sprig of fashion was not a coachman, but a young buck. I collect he wants to become a member of the Four-in-Hand Club."

Fancy shook her head. "I do not understand."

"It's all the rage now for a young buck to learn how to drive a coach. They often pay the regular coachman for the privilege. Mr. Akers had his front teeth filed and paid one Dick Vaughan, alias 'Hell-Fire Dick,' £50 to teach him how to spit properly."

"Ugh!" Fancy shivered. "The members of the *ton* are a strange lot."

Castleford smiled. "Don't be too hard on the young bucks. They have to have some adventure in their lives. The Grand Tour has been impossible since all this trouble with Bony and the young ones haven't enough to do with their energies."

Fancy raised an expressive eyebrow. "There must be something more useful they could do."

Castleford shook his head. "Young blood is hot. They may kick up a spree in the wee hours and overturn the Charlies in their boxes."

"But the watchmen are there to protect *them!*"

Castleford shrugged. "Or they may get up a match with a pugilist, or learn fencing at Master Angelo's School of Arms. They may game away whatever allowances their fond papas settle upon them, either at one of the clubs or at a 'hell' or at the races. There are cock fights, bear baiting, and Billy the Terrier is reputed to be able to dispatch upwards of 100 rats in an hour."

"Oh, stop," cried Fancy. "All those things sound dreadful. Blood and pain—oh! Just savage! How can they call themselves gentlemen?"

Castleford made a face. "I don't know. But they do. Of course, we also have more civilized amusements, of the kind that Morgane and I now favor. The opera, the theater."

Fancy smiled. "And the pursuit of bits of muslin?"

The Marquis chuckled. "Perhaps, on occasion. But Morgane and I are really theater enthusiasts. For instance, we are greatly looking forward to seeing *Every Man in His Humour*. We always attend, too, when the great Kemble or Mrs. Siddons is to perform. It is the one disaster of our lives that we were born too late to see the immortal Garrick."

Fancy nodded. She could understand such a desire, for she, too, had often longed to see some of the greats of bygone days.

135

"What do you think of Uncle—of Cooke?" she asked curiously.

"The man's quite an actor," replied Castleford. "Especially in roles like *Richard III*. He plays evil to perfection. But—" he hesitated, as though sparing her feelings.

"Go on," said Fancy. "Tell me what you truly think."

"He is overly fond of blue ruin. If he were not so good, he would have been kept off the stage before this. Is he important to you?"

Fancy nodded. "He was my mama's friend. Ever since I was a tiny little girl I've called him Uncle George."

"That explains your defense of him that night."

"Yes." Fancy heaved a sigh. "And I know he drinks too much and keeps bad company, but there's nothing I can do to help him."

Castleford nodded sagely. "Well, perhaps he will come to his senses before it is too late."

Fancy did not put much faith in such a hope, but, since she knew the Marquis was trying to cheer her up, she did not say so.

"Ah," said Castleford with a smile of satisfaction, "there is Prinny."

"The Prince of Wales? Where?" asked Fancy.

"Over there in the flaring yellow barouche with Lady Hertford."

Fancy could not help staring. The Prince of Wales had been much talked about at Bath, though he seldom came there. The seashore was his favorite and there was much talk of that magnificent pavilion at Brighton. But the Prince did not seem princely to Fancy, whose ideals of royalty were based on the theater. His Royal Highness's corpulence distressed her. His sumptuous clothes could not hide his bulk. And the plump and matronly woman beside him looked exactly like someone's grandmother.

"Why," cried Fancy in disappointment, "he's fat!"

"Hush." Castleford looked a little worried. "Miss Harper, we don't say things like that about our sovereign-to-be."

Fancy frowned. "I don't know what good that does. Not saying anything isn't going to make him any leaner."

Castleford smiled as the Prince's carriage passed out of sight. "Perhaps not, but it will keep us in his good graces. Prinny is not a bad sort, but like all royalty he doesn't take well to insult. Only Beau Brummell can do that with impunity. Only the Beau has that much nerve."

"Is *he* here?" asked Fancy.

Castleford quickly surveyed the park—or as much of it as he could see through the rapidly rising dust. "I don't see him anywhere. He probably left early. The dust plays the devil with his looks. What's the use of a man spending three or four hours to get his cravat tied just right if he's going to get it dusty right off?"

Fancy's forehead wrinkled in distaste. What a

waste it seemed. All that time just to get dressed. "It doesn't take me that long to get into makeup for a play," she replied. "Milord, are there no gentlemen who devote themselves to anything worthwhile?"

Castleford considered this for several minutes. "Yes, I suppose there are."

"What do they do?"

"Well, some are very concerned with business in the House, passing bills, and such. And some have taken to managing their own estates instead of leaving them in the hands of stewards. But that takes a good deal of time, managing rent rolls and all. Ask Morgane sometime. He does that."

"He manages his own estates?"

"Yes, though it takes him a devil of a lot of work. He's always visiting this one or that one. I tell him it leaves him little time for the gaming tables—and the ladybirds. But then, he was never much of a gamester, not Morgane. Not that he didn't have the nerve for it. Never saw a cooler man anywhere. He just said it was boring." Castleford grinned. "On the other hand, he's always had an eye out for the ladybirds—and they for him."

Fancy found that she did not like this piece of information, though why she should care anything about the Earl's personal life and habits she had no idea. He certainly meant nothing to her. Nothing at all.

The dust was getting wearisome and the sun seemed to have gone behind some clouds. Fancy sighed. "I am getting rather tired, Castleford. Could we please go home?"

"Of course, Miss Harper. Of course. I didn't mean to fatigue you."

Fancy managed a smile. "You have not fatigued me. I have been working rather hard learning my lines and the drive was good for me. But I find that I am tired now."

Castleford gave the necessary orders and not long afterward Fancy found herself deposited at her door. "I hope you will accompany me again soon," said the Marquis.

"Thank you," replied Fancy. "You are most kind."

As she turned to pass through the door that Henry held for her, Castleford spoke again. "I shall be in our box for *Every Man in His Humour* and hope that the audience will behave itself."

"Thank you, milord."

As Henry closed the door behind her, he spoke softly. "He seems a nice sort, the Marquis."

"Very nice," said Fancy with a smile as she removed the new straw bonnet and trudged up the stairs. Castleford was indeed very nice, but it was the sardonic face of the dark Earl that kept appearing in her mind at the oddest moments. He was impossible, that man, intruding, she thought angrily, even into her thoughts!

Chapter Nine

The next Wednesday evening found an excited Fancy in her dressing room again. She had rehearsed till she knew her lines to perfection and now she looked forward eagerly to the moment when she would face the audience as Mrs. Kitely. She only hoped that the rioters would be not so much in evidence.

Though the members of the company, including Fancy, were becoming a little more accustomed to the continued clamor, she couldn't help wishing that for a change she might give a performance that could be heard.

As the players began to gather, Fancy looked around for Cooke. When the time for curtain call grew nearer and nearer, Fancy's anxiety increased. Oh, she begged silently, Uncle George couldn't be bosky this night. There was never any way of knowing how—or even when—he was going to show up.

Fancy suppressed a sigh. George Cooke was a difficult man to care about. She saw the young actress Annie glance her way and elevate her pert nose in distaste. With difficulty Fancy refrained from scowling back. Until the intrusion of the Earl into the greenroom she and Annie had gotten along quite well. For in spite of her fiery hair Fancy was usually quite even-tempered. But since the evening that the Earl had snubbed her, Annie had not had as much as a hello for her rival. Another place where the Earl was intruding in her life, and as always, she thought grimly, altering it for the worse.

Well, she was not going to let Annie spoil the evening, no more than she would let the Earl.

From her place in the wings Fancy surveyed the audience. They did not look too riotously inclined, though the hum of noise was incessant and here and there O.P. placards and banners were apparent. Fancy picked out the burly forms of several pugilists scattered here and there in the pit. She raised her eyes to scan the boxes, unconsciously letting them skim over the one that Castleford shared with his friend Morgane. The two were not yet in their seats, but Fancy knew from experience that they would arrive at the theater. Why they should want to see the same play three or four nights running, she could not imagine. But she knew that they had been there every night since the ruffians had almost carried her away. And so it seemed quite likely that they would be there this night also.

A slight commotion in another part of the theater caused her to turn her attention in that direction. His Royal Highness, the Duke of York, was being ushered to his seat by the theater managers. Bareheaded and carrying lighted candles they led York to his box.

Fancy stifled a sigh. She supposed it had been too much to hope that the Duke would forget about her. She did not want to offend royalty, but she knew she would remain adamant in her decision to have no protector. And all this would not help her any with the rest of the company. No one would understand her refusing the attentions of a man who could bring the theater so much patronage.

They would think it foolish, even stupid, of her to turn down an offer from such a man. The recent scandal had not tarnished his image among the players. After all, a world in which intangible things were sold was familiar to them. This man sold his talent, that man his influence. A person had to get by the best way possible. And no one would condemn Fancy for selling her beauty in this fashion. Indeed, they would think it strange if she didn't. Annie, in particular, would be sure to circulate nasty stories of some kind.

Moving back from the curtain, Fancy shrugged.

Annie's animosity was nothing new. Many an aspiring actress had envied Fancy her looks and her talent. But she had always managed to stay cool and go on her own way. Now, of course, she had the Earl to deal with and Annie's pinpricks were so many little annoyances added to the big one.

Just then a small bustle to the side of the stage attracted her attention. With relief Fancy saw that Cooke had arrived. His gait was steady enough, but she was too far away to see his eyes. Sometimes he looked like this, perfectly capable, and then right in the middle of the performance the alcohol would hit him like a great blow. All she could do was hope that this was not to be one of those nights.

Some time later, when she returned to the dressing room during the intermission, she was still hoping. She did not like the blue-ruin gleam in his eye, but so far his performance had been adequate. Sometimes he could even be heard above the clamor of the rioters.

With a sigh Fancy plopped onto a stool to examine her makeup, and there on her dressing table lay not one but two notes. With trembling fingers she picked up the first and tore it open. His Royal Highness, the Duke of York, would be pleased to have her as his guest at a small private supper after the performance, she read.

Fancy's shoulders drooped dispiritedly. For a moment she wished herself rid of such troublesome beauty. But common sense soon asserted itself. She

143

must think of some excuse to offer York, but for the moment she would read her other note.

There was no need to look for the signature at the bottom. The bold heavy strokes of the pen left no doubt in her mind that the writer of this note was the arrogant Earl. "I have something of importance to discuss with you privately. Wait for me in your dressing room after the performance."

Fancy stiffened. How very like the Earl! No consideration as to her feelings in the matter. Not even a please. Well, the top-lofty Earl would have to learn that Fancy Harper was not a woman to be pushed around.

But there was still the problem of York. How could she refuse a royal duke's invitation to supper? Absently, Fancy fingered the two notes.

Then hastily she grabbed up a pen and began to write. To York she conveyed her regrets that she had already accepted an invitation to supper with Morgane. And to Morgane she sent a curt "I do not wish to see you."

That should keep them both quiet, she thought firmly. Even if York saw her leaving in her own carriage, he would merely assume that, since Morgane lived next door, she was meeting him later.

With a quick glance at the mirror, Fancy hurried out to the greenroom, where she motioned to the boy who ran errands and gave him instructions. Then it was time to return to the stage.

As the play progressed Fancy's nerves grew raw. Time and time again Cooke faltered and barely recovered. Whenever possible Fancy fed him his lines. At other times the prompter tried, but his words were difficult to hear over the clamor.

And then the crowd began what had been called the O.P. war dance. It began slowly, then swelled into more and more noise, ending in a confusion almost demonical. Rhythmically the crowd clapped, stamped their feet, beat on the benches, while they steadily chanted, "O.P., O.P."

More than once Fancy feared that Cooke would turn and denounce the audience. But fortunately the play drew to its close and he even managed to make his last exit.

Fancy felt literally exhausted. Every player knew that it was difficult to carry a fellow performer. When that person was someone you cared about, the toll was even more exhausting.

With a sigh Fancy settled once more at her dressing table. Thank goodness she had solved the problem of York's invitation, she thought, as she began to remove makeup. And as for the haughty Earl of Morgane, perhaps he would take the hint and leave her in peace!

She had cleansed her face, removed her costume, and slipped into her own gown when a brisk knock sounded on the door. Without much thought Fancy called, "Come in."

She regretted her words instantly for the door opened to admit the Earl. He smiled sardonically as he stepped in and closed the door behind him.

Fancy felt her temper building. She rose from

the stool and faced him. "I wrote that I do not wish to see you," she cried angrily.

Morgane's eyes glittered with amusement. "So you did. But *I* wished to see you. So—" He shrugged eloquently.

Fancy found that her hands had curled into fists. How terribly top-lofty the Earl could be! "I do not wish to see you," she repeated. "Please leave my dressing room."

The Earl smiled, that sardonic smile that reflected no warmth whatsoever. "I have something to speak to you about. I do not think it—"

Another knock sounded and the door opened to admit a beaming Duke of York. Fancy's heart rose in her throat. If York said something about her supposed supper with Morgane, she would really be in the suds.

The Duke continued to smile as he surveyed Fancy through his quizzing glass. "You were lovely tonight, my dear," said he.

"Thank you, Your Highness," faltered Fancy.

"I simply came to be assured that you were in good hands."

"Very good hands, sir," remarked the Earl urbanely. "We were just discussing a rather personal matter."

Fancy bridled and was about to snap out that she had nothing of a personal nature to discuss with him, and never would, when she remembered her note and held her tongue. With York looking

146

at her questioningly, Fancy managed to nod. The Duke continued to smile. He was a man not easily disconcerted.

"Well," he observed heartily. "Enjoy yourself, Morgane. You have taken the field—for tonight at least. But there will be other encounters."

As the door closed behind him, Fancy swallowed a sigh of relief. And then she was aware of Morgane's cool eyes boring into hers. For long moments they stood silent, eyes locked. Desperately Fancy strove to wrench her eyes free, but something compelled her to remain locked in his gaze.

It was the Earl who finally broke the silence. "Where is your cloak? We can talk on the way home."

"Home!"

Morgane nodded. "Come, my horses will grow tired of waiting."

Fancy fought with an intense desire to assault the Earl physically with her fists. "I am not going home with you," she said from between clenched teeth.

The Earl continued to smile. "I fear you are mistaken, my dear. You and I are supposed to be having a light supper together. Have you forgotten so soon? I am wounded to the core."

Not for years had Fancy had such a desire to stamp her foot and scream, to throw something— anything. With great effort she controlled herself.

She would not give the arrogant Earl the chance to laugh at her. "I fear the mistake is yours, milord," she replied icily.

Morgane shook his head. "Not so. I have it on the best authority that you are planning to sup with me."

"What authority?"

The Earl's eyes glittered with sardonic amusement. "The next time you send York a note saying that you plan to take supper with me, best make sure that I am not by when it is delivered."

Fancy bit her lip in vexation. "But I sent you a note, too."

Morgane nodded. "Yes, some rubbish about not desiring to see me. But how could that be?" He smiled devilishly. "His Royal Highness looked up from his missive and congratulated me on having supper with you. You would not have wished me to express surprise, I presume."

Fancy shook her head in aggravation. "I do not want to have supper with either of you."

"But you did not tell York that."

"I—I did not wish to offend him."

"I see." The Earl gazed at her speculatively. "I presume that you felt no such regret at offending me."

"Of course not," replied Fancy quite honestly and was amazed to hear the Earl burst into laughter.

"You are a strange creature, Miss Fancy Harper. But come, where is your cloak?"

148

"I am going home in my own carriage as I planned," asserted Fancy.

Morgane shook his head. "I should not do such a foolish thing if I were you," he commented evenly.

"What is foolish about it?" demanded an angry Fancy.

"His Royal Highness will discover that you lied to him and he will be doubly offended."

"He will not discover anything," said Fancy defiantly, reaching for her bonnet. "If he says anything, I will simply tell him that I am taking my own carriage home. Since we are neighbors that should serve."

"You have forgotten one important factor," said the Earl.

Fancy frowned. "What is that?"

"Me."

"Will you stop this flummery," cried Fancy, "and tell me what you are talking about?"

"It is really quite simple. I desire your company—uncomfortable as it so often is. You have informed York that we will be together."

"But that was to get rid of him!"

The Earl nodded somberly. "And quite well done, too." His mouth hardened. "I, however, am not easily gotten rid of. You will either come home in my carriage or I go straightway to York and tell him the truth about your ruse."

"You wouldn't!"

"You mistake me, Miss Harper. I very much would. I always get what I want. And I am not

149

averse to using somewhat unpleasant methods of acquiring it."

"Oh!" Fancy clenched her fists till her nails dug into her palms. "You are a detestable creature," she cried. "The most reprehensible man I have ever known."

The Earl smiled sardonically. "At the least, I have gained some distinction in your eyes."

"Oh!" Fancy came very close to stamping her foot, but fear of the ridicule she would see in his eyes restrained her. "I shall not be very good company," she snapped.

The Earl bowed slightly. "You forget, my dear. I have seen you at your worst, not once, but several times. I must admit you are not the best companion around, but I will feast my eyes on your beauty and so in part compensate myself for your terrible temper."

"I do not have a terrible temper!" It was with the greatest difficulty that Fancy kept herself from proving just the opposite. At that moment she would have given anything in the world to throw something at the urbanely smiling face of the arrogant Earl.

"Come, come," he repeated. "I don't doubt that York is waiting in the greenroom to see us depart together. A hunter like York doesn't give up the chase easily."

Fancy slammed the bonnet on her head and tied the ribbons savagely under her chin. Then she snatched up her cloak and started toward the door. Morgane's cool voice detained her.

"May I suggest, Miss Harper, that you achieve some degree of complaisance in your features before we leave this room? You are, after all, an actress. This should be a minor chore for you."

Fancy glowered at him. "I despise you," she hissed.

"Quite within your rights," agreed Morgane cheerfully. "But if you expect to deceive York you'll have to hide it. We are supposed to be enroute to a little tête-à-tête, not my murder."

Fancy turned her back on him and took several deep breaths. As horrible as the man was, she had to concede that he was right. But pretending to have pleasant feelings for one she considered the most despicable person of her acquaintance would probably be the most difficult acting role she had ever attempted.

For a few moments Fancy concentrated, using all her resources. Then she turned and smiled sweetly. "I am quite ready to go home now, milord. Thank you."

Morgane chuckled. "Admirably done. And now" —he offered her his arm—"let us proceed to my carriage so that the strain on you will not be too great."

Some moments later Fancy settled back against the velvet squabs of the Earl's closed carriage. It had, she could not help noticing, his coat of arms painted on the door and was, as carriages go, undoubtedly one of the best. This thought did little to mollify her. A coach completely made of gold could not do that.

She had kept the smile on her face as they passed the greenroom and exited through the crowds to where the Earl's carriage stood waiting, but she smiled no longer. The Earl could force her to ride home with him. He could not force her to be pleasant!

As he settled on the squabs beside her and the carriage moved forward into the crowded street, Fancy held herself in readiness. Because she had been tricked into riding in his carriage did not mean that she would let him take any liberties with her person. And she intended for him to know that!

"You need not hold yourself so stiffly," remarked the Earl. "I have never found it necessary to use force." He turned to face her and in the light of the carriage lamps she saw him smile. "In fact, you are the first woman to have refused me." He paused as though considering. "Perhaps it is that that piques me so."

"I do not see what pleasure you can get from persecuting me," Fancy declared.

The Earl looked surprised. "Is that not rather strong language? I simply desire your company."

"To bait me!" Fancy cried.

Morgane shook his head. "I had thought I was offering you worthwhile advice, not insult. The theater is not the place for innocents." He raised an eyebrow. "If you *are* the innocent you declare you are."

Fancy glared at him. "I do not lie."

"Softly, softly. Has it not occurred to you that I might be legitimately concerned for your happiness?"

Fancy was about to snap out an angry no, but suddenly she stopped, her anger strangely dissipated. "I'm afraid it has not," she said evenly, not sure if this were another trick of the Earl's.

"I think it may be conceded by the *ton* that I am not a complete blackguard. You are young and beautiful. In the theater you will always be subject to the advances of men of wealth and position. Such is the nature of the world. Sooner or later you will succumb and lose that innocence which you value so highly."

Fancy shook her head. "I think not, milord. Perhaps you do not understand how I feel about the theater. It's a world apart, a world of beauty and truth."

"It is a world of tinsel and illusion," replied Morgane in the same even tone. "You are deluding yourself by thinking otherwise. Since women first took to the stage after the Restoration they have used it as a marketplace for puffing themselves."

"But I am not like that," Fancy protested. "I love the theater for itself. We make people happy; we entertain them."

The Earl shrugged. "And then they go back to

the same life of ennui. You would do better to 'entertain' in another fashion."

Fancy felt herself bristling up again. "There have been greats in the theater: Garrick, Kemble, Peg Woffington, Kitty Clive, Mrs. Siddons."

"I do not presume to speak of Mrs. Siddons's private life," interposed the Earl, "but that of Woffington and Clive was certainly of the very kind you disdain."

Fancy shook her head. "You don't understand. I don't *care* about their private lives. They were great *actresses*. They gave themselves to the theater."

"And the point *I* wish to make is that they did not find it necessary to forgo certain other aspects of life."

Fancy's heart began to pound. "I do not wish to marry," she said firmly. "I do not wish to have a protector. I am perfectly capable of taking care of myself."

The Earl smiled dryly. "For one so innocent you are dreadfully cynical. Is it not possible for an actress to form an attachment or make a connection for other than mercenary purposes?"

Fancy glared at him. "Of course it is possible."

"But not in your case."

Fancy nodded. "I do not find the company of men very satisfying," she said quite bluntly.

Morgane chuckled. "I believe you are guilty of somewhat faulty reasoning. Never having formed

154

an attachment for a man how can you honestly say you would not like it?"

Fancy shrugged. "I do not care about reasoning—faulty or otherwise. I only know what I want."

"Or don't want."

"Can't you understand how I might love the theater?" asked Fancy. "Have you no overwhelming abiding interest in something?"

The Earl regarded her for long moments, his eyes gleaming strangely in the light of the carriage lamps. "Yes," he said finally, a slight smile twisting his thin lips. "I want to have what I want."

The warmth in his eyes so unnerved Fancy that she felt herself coloring up. "In this world," she said stiffly, "it is not always possible to have what one wants."

The Earl shrugged. "So they told me as a child. But somehow I always persisted until I got what I wanted."

"Exce—" Fancy stopped suddenly. She must not mention that old duel; she had promised Castleford. "Except that no one can *always* do that."

The Earl's gray eyes were strangely golden in the lamplight as they met hers. "I have so far been quite successful."

"So far," said Fancy with a shake of her head that plainly reflected her disbelief.

The Earl chuckled. "You are not yet convinced. Ah well, time is of little moment to the young. But at two and thirty one begins to experience impatience. Nevertheless, I am a man who can wait."

Something inside Fancy trembled as she heard this. It seemed that the Earl was saying very clearly that he meant to get *her*. But, as he did not expound any further on this subject, she went back to her defense of the theater.

"The theater is good. We make people laugh. For a while they escape their troubles. And I have fun. I can be many different people."

"And escape the emptiness of your life," observed the Earl dryly.

"My life is *not* empty," returned Fancy hotly.

"No, no doubt you give some affection to that creature misnamed a dog."

"Oh! You have not listened to what I am telling you!"

"*Au contraire,*" drawled the Earl. "I have heard every word, but the unmistakable fact remains. If you are an actress, men will wish to keep you. Such is the nature of the beast."

Fancy, remembering the occasion of her first meeting with the Earl, grew even angrier. "That is their problem, not mine."

"I hesitate to disagree with you," said the Earl cheerfully, "but you are mistaken. Right now, for instance, many will have assumed that I have already achieved my purpose."

For a horrid moment Fancy sat in silence. "But you haven't!"

The Earl chuckled dryly. "But only you and I,

my dear, are aware of that. York thinks we are having an intimate tête-à-tête, a little supper for two. And he will naturally believe that it will be followed by more."

"Oh!" Fancy's hands clenched into fists. "You are a beast!"

The Earl's eyes darkened. "I should control my anger, if I were you. My own temper is easily ignited."

Fancy heard the warning, even guessed what it might portend, but she could no longer suppress her rage. "I despise you," she cried. "You are an impossible person. If ever I had any inclination toward 'affection,' which thank God I have not, your acquaintance would be enough to turn me away."

The Earl's eyes glittered dangerously, but Fancy was too far gone to care. "I find your company distasteful and your kisses absolutely odious. I should never—"

This last was cut off quite suddenly as Fancy found herself caught in a brutal embrace. The Earl was quite strong and fight as she would she could not hope to escape him in the confines of the coach. Still she struggled silently until one of his hands forced her chin up and his lips possessed hers.

It was a savage kiss, harsh and full of unrestrained passion, passion such as she had never experienced. To her dismay Fancy found something in herself responding to it. For one unfor-

157

gettable moment her lips softened under his. Just as suddenly as he had grabbed her the Earl thrust her away from him.

"Your lips may form words that reject me," he said, breathing hard. "But under mine they do not lie."

Fancy marshaled her defenses. "You are mistaken, milord. Perhaps so much success with the fair ones has turned your head."

The Earl laughed savagely and Fancy shrank away from him. "Perhaps," he said. "But I have had much experience with the frail sex. And no woman who ever returned my kiss like that failed at last to come to my arms."

Fancy, whose heart was still beating in her throat, gave him a disdainful glance. "Then, milord, I shall have the distinction of being the first."

It seemed for a moment as though he might reach for her again and somewhere inside her Fancy was aware of a terrible desire to have him do so.

But fortunately for her pride the carriage came to a halt. Morgane smiled. "We have reached your residence and so you are safe—for tonight," he said as he handed her out.

"I should think a man like you would be too proud to force a woman," cried Fancy hotly.

The Earl smiled darkly as he left her at the open door. "I shall not force you, my dear. I assure you of that. When the time comes, you will come quite willingly to my arms."

Chapter Ten

━━━━━━━━━━━━━━━━━━━━━━━━━━━━━━━━━━━━━

Fancy's feelings of rage at the Earl were little
abated when she rose several days later. The run of
Every Man in His Humour was over, but she had
to prepare for her part in *The Blind Boy*. There
was a great deal to be done. Still, she could not
banish the thought of the Earl's angry kiss from her
mind.

She had been kissed before, and, on occasion,
she had found it pleasant enough. But never before
had she felt her insides melting away like that nor
her heart pounding in her throat. Morgane was a
man experienced with women. There was no doubt
about that. And he knew how to kiss.

At this point Fancy tossed her head disdainfully
and reached for a morning dress of orange-sprigged
muslin. So, the Earl knew how to kiss. That was

159

certainly no concern of hers. She had no intention of forming any sort of connection with a man. No intention at all.

Fancy gazed critically at her reflection in the cheval glass. She was looking a little hagged these days. With a sigh she turned away and went down to breakfast.

Since this was Sunday there were no rehearsals and a long day stretched ahead of her. Full of things to be done, of course, but boding to be lonely. At the theater there were always people about, someone to talk to. And most of them were very nice people. Of course, there were a few like that little snip Annie. Undoubtedly she would have something to say about the relatively small part that Fancy had in *The Blind Boy*.

Fancy made a face. If the great Peg Woffington had been willing to take small parts as well as the leads, then certainly Fancy Harper would not wrinkle up her nose at them. Of course, Fancy knew that if she had refused the part, it might very well have gone to Annie. And Annie knew that too. But Fancy couldn't help it. If Mr. Kemble asked her to play a part, she would play it.

As the day wore on she went through her lines for *The Blind Boy*. From time to time she stopped to cast an appreciative eye at some architectural feature of the drawing room. That was one thing she could thank the Earl for, Fancy told herself with a grin. She now had a much better apprecia-

160

tion of the beauties of her home. And was even more determined not to leave it!

It was well into calling hours when a brisk rap from the knocker sent Henry to the front door. Fancy, listening in the drawing room, heard Castleford's hearty tones and smiled. Here was someone to talk to.

She went to meet him. "Castleford, how nice to see you."

The Marquis seemed surprised at this warm welcome, but he lost no time in taking advantage of it. "My dear Miss Harper," he cried, taking Fancy's hand in his. "I am so pleased to find you at home."

"I do not do much visiting," said Fancy with amusement. "And since we are not rehearsing today—"

"Of course, of course." Releasing her hand, Castleford looked around the drawing room. "Nice place you've got here."

Fancy nodded and found that she could not resist the temptation to pass on her new knowledge. "It was built by Robert Adam in the last century. Notice how he designed this room—even the paintings and carpet—to make a perfect unity."

For a moment Castleford stared at her in dismay. Then he clapped his big hand to his forehead. "Please, Miss Harper, I beg of you. Whatever more you know of Robert Adam's work do not grace me with the information."

The Marquis sighed heavily. "I happen to have

a Robert Adam house, every inch of which has been explained to me in the most intricate detail. I tell you, I am about ready to put the place up for sale. Just so I may not have to hear anymore about the great Adam."

Fancy laughed. "I collect it is your friend the Earl who so enlightens you."

Castleford nodded. "Yes, I suppose he must have done it to you, too. Isn't it the most aggravating thing? As though one may not enjoy his house without all that nonsense about chiaroscuro and such."

"I personally like the effects of light and shade evidenced—" At the look of utter dismay on Castleford's face Fancy broke into peals of laughter. "All right, Castleford, I collect the Earl has troubled you with that, too."

"Indeed, he has," sighed the Marquis. "He's an admirable man, Morgane. And my best friend. But he's deep. Sometimes he's too deep for me."

Fancy was tempted to inform Castleford that his friend was also ill tempered and top-lofty, but she thought better of it. "What brought you calling today? Has the *ennui* caught up with you?" she asked.

Castleford shook his head and took a step toward her.

"Won't you be seated, milord?" said Fancy, quickly dropping into a chair.

As Castleford drew up a dainty chair that made his great form seem even bulkier, his face took on a most somber expression. "I have come to speak to you on a matter of some importance."

Fancy nodded. From the serious look on the Marquis's face it must be a matter of great importance.

"You remember that I told you I have been thinking lately of settling down?"

"Because of your advanced age of two and thirty," said Fancy with a smile.

Castleford did not smile in return. "Yes. I am getting on in years and it is time for me to choose a bride."

"Have you a particular lady in mind?" asked Fancy curiously.

The Marquis nodded. "Oh, yes. She is quite beautiful—and accomplished. And of good character. I am sure of it."

"Castleford, I congratulate you. You will certainly be happy with such a paragon."

The Marquis smiled sheepishly. "My happiness lies in your hands."

"Mine!"

"Yes. I have come today—" He paused and then, gathering his courage, plunged on. "I have come to make you an offer. Of marriage," he hastened to add.

Fancy sat in numb silence. "Castleford, you can't marry an actress," she said finally. "Think of your family."

"They might not take it kindly at first. But after they got to know you, they'd come round."

"Castleford, are you all about in your head?"

The Marquis reddened. "Of course not. You will make a very beautiful marchioness."

For a moment Fancy considered this, but it was too much to imagine. "Castleford, I cannot be a marchioness. I do not know how. I am an actress, not a lady."

"You can hold your own with the best of ladies," said Castleford firmly. "And my family will receive you. I guarantee that."

Fancy shook her head. "I am greatly honored, milord. Greatly. But I cannot accept."

"I'll settle a good jointure on you," declared Castleford. "This house and your income. It will all be yours. And pin money, too."

Fancy shook her head. "Milord, listen to me. Listen carefully. You are a very nice man. I like you. But I do not wish to marry. Truly I do not. And you know in your heart that such a marriage would not set well with your family. Think of them."

"I should rather think of myself," said Castleford. "For if I don't, no one else will. And I want you. I have a lot to offer you, including my affection. And I am persuaded we should deal famously together."

"But Castleford, you see," cried Fancy, fastening on this information, "that is the problem. I should never marry for money—only if I had formed a partiality for the man. And much as I respect and admire you, I have not that kind of feeling for you."

Castleford sighed. "I believe you, Miss Harper. And I rather thought you'd say something like this, but I felt I couldn't do any damage by trying. We are still friends, are we not?"

"Of course we are," said Fancy gently. "Good friends."

"Well," said the Marquis, "that is some consolation. If I cannot have you as dasher or wife then I suppose I must settle for friend."

Fancy chuckled at this forthright statement and rose to escort the Marquis to the door.

"May I still come sometimes to call or take you for a ride in Hyde Park?" he asked sheepishly as he clapped his beaver on his head and received his gloves and cane from Henry.

"Of course," replied Fancy with a smile. "Remember, we are friends."

"Yes, friends." Then the Marquis was down the steps and into his carriage.

As Henry closed the door and turned to face her Fancy laughed. "I have come up in the world, Henry. The Marquis of Castleford has made me an honorable offer—of marriage. I refused him, of course. But I could have been a marchioness. Imagine that."

Henry smiled. "I rather think the Marquis, though he might marry an actress, would not wish her to continue in such a line of work."

"I don't suppose he would either," said Fancy with a grin. "But in any case, we shall never know definitely—for I shall never be a marchioness."

And with that Fancy returned to her drawing room and her script to walk once more through her lines.

But the surprises that this day was to bring her were not yet over. It was no more than ten minutes before the sound of the knocker was heard again.

Fancy felt her heart rise up in her throat. Could Morgane have seen his friend's carriage and come to remonstrate with her? Her hand flew to her mouth in dismay. With the Earl's kiss still so strongly in her mind she had no wish to see him.

But the tones that reached her ears were not the deep vibrant ones of Morgane's voice. With a start Fancy recognized the tones of His Royal Highness, the Duke of York. What could he be doing here?

There was no time for more thinking because York was upon her. "My dear Miss Harper," he boomed. "How well you are looking."

Fancy could not forbear a small smile of amusement. So York, at least, did not find her hagged.

"Good day, Your Royal Highness, won't you sit down?"

York sighed and ran a hand through his fair hair now tinged with gray. He settled in a chair; the same one, Fancy could not help noticing, that

Castleford had used. At his gesture she dropped into hers.

"I am a blunt man," said York. "Always have been. Best way to behave."

Fancy nodded. That was certainly sensible. But it was suddenly borne upon her that the Duke looked strangely serious. With a sinking heart she formed a quick conjecture as to his errand, but she saw no way to forestall him.

"I'll go right to the point. You've heard about the Clarke business." He shook his head. "That woman disappointed me, sadly. I trusted her. Imagine her adding names to the lists." The Duke looked so forlorn that Fancy was more than ever assured of his innocence. "At any rate, I have sent her packing. And I'm looking to form a new connection."

"I am an actress," said Fancy. "Not a convenience."

"Don't have no mind to get your back up," said he cheerfully. "Like I said, I'm a blunt man. And I've never seen a high-flyer with the looks you've got. The Clarke was a dark beauty but yours is like fire."

"Your Royal Highness," said Fancy. "I have not got my back up. But I am not the sort of woman you suppose me to be. I am an actress. The theater is my life."

"I don't figure to meddle in that," said York quite reasonably. "My brother William has lived

happily with his Mrs. Jordan for many years—
whenever he's home from the seas. And often
enough it seems by the number of FitzClarences
around. And he didn't mind her being on the stage.
Indeed," said he with a dry smile, "we're in somewhat similar shakes as far as blunt is concerned.
There's no use me pretending I can set you up in
any tremendous great style. I'm a gamester and I
never have enough of the ready. But I can give you
a lot of patronage. And I'm not a complete pinch-
penny."

Apparently satisfied that he had had his say,
York leaned back in his chair with a sigh.

Fancy, fighting an inclination to giggle, gave
him a small smile. "I am not offended at your
bluntness, sir, but I do not want to form a connection, not of any kind. I am very happy, you
see, just as I am."

The Duke shook his head. "I collect the Earl is
giving me some competition."

"Indeed not!" cried Fancy hastily. "I have no
partiality for any man."

"Good," said York, rising suddenly. "In that case
I will not give up hope. Perhaps at some later date
I shall resume my suit. And now I must go. My
brother expects me at Carlton House and I have a
new nag I must look over first."

He raised Fancy's fingers to his lips and beamed
down at her. "No need to go to the door with me,
my dear." He glanced down at the script that lay

on the table. "I'm sure you've work to do. I'll look forward to seeing you again soon."

With another smile the Duke exited. For a long moment Fancy stared at the carved figures in the panel above the fireplace, stared without seeing. Then she dropped silently into a chair. Well, this had certainly been a day.

First an offer of marriage—to a marquis yet. And now—an offer to be a royal mistress. Which, thought a bemused Fancy, should be considered the best offer?

She was still considering this rather hypothetical question when Ethel's voice came cutting through the room. "So—now York's been here."

Fancy nodded. "I suppose Henry told you about Castleford."

Ethel advanced into the room and nodded. "Didn't he though. Seeing as how York already has a wife I suppose it was something else *he* was offering you," Ethel remarked dourly.

Fancy's eyes began to sparkle. "Yes, Ethel. He wants to be my protector. Sit down and discuss this with me. Which do you think is the better offer?"

Ethel had not spent twenty years with her young mistress without being aware of her mischievous streak and merely frowned. "Ain't no use you asking me them addlepated questions," she said. "I know you ain't forming no connection with neither of them. If you was, I'd say the Marquis was your best bet. Ain't no little thing to be a marchioness. And it's legal like. But then you'd lose the stage 'cause I don't doubt he'd mean to do you up proper. On the other hand, if we was poor in the pocket and not plump as this place makes us and you was set on keeping to the stage, then York would be best. But since we ain't near starving and you ain't got no feeling for neither of 'em, then I think you done right in refusing them both."

Fancy sprang from her chair and gave the surprised woman a great hug. "As usual, Ethel, you are quite right. But it was rather pleasant to be asked and it has set me up no end." She patted at her hair. "Don't you think I look less hagged?"

"You ain't never been hagged," said Ethel, "since the day you was born. And if you ask me—which you ain't—I'd say I knows quite well *who* it is puts that sparkle in your eye."

Before Fancy could summon words to deny this outrageous statement Henry coughed discreetly from the doorway. "I'm sorry, Miss Fancy, but the dog — he sneaked out when the Duke left."

"Oh, no!" Fancy would have liked to let go on someone but prudently kept her tongue between her teeth. Henry could not be supposed to attend to everything and the dog was always waiting by the door.

"I sent the footman after him. You know, Benson."

Fancy nodded. "Will he come home with him?"

Henry shook his head. "I don't know. If he don't, mayhap the Earl will bring him."

"Oh, no!" repeated Fancy. "I cannot stand to have that abominable man in my house again."

Ethel uttered a sound that greatly resembled a snort and marched off muttering about speaking to that Frenchman so he would prepare a decent dinner.

Henry, taking a look at Fancy's flushed countenance, offered a few soothing words. "The Earl ain't such a bad sort—really. I mean—it would set any man's back up to have a great dog like that throwing himself against a new door."

"Henry," said Fancy with considerable acerbity. "Do not speak to me of the Earl. He is an abominable top-lofty odious creature and I have no wish to see him."

"In that case," said a deep voice from the doorway, "I suggest that you do something about *this* odious creature." As the Earl entered the room, leading Hercules, who was wagging his great tail, Fancy felt her cheeks flood scarlet. She rose quickly. "I am truly sorry. Hercules sneaked out when the D—when one of my callers left."

The Earl smiled sardonically. "May I suggest to you that for the present your butler might dispose of this giant?"

Fancy looked helplessly toward Henry. But that worthy was already quietly taking the rope from the Earl's hand and leading Hercules away.

For a moment Fancy stood in silence. "It is customary to ask a visiting gentleman to be

171

seated," said the Earl in a tone quite above reproach.

Fancy bridled anyway. "I was not aware that you were *were* a visitor," she said harshly.

The Earl did not seem to take umbrage at this. He merely settled himself, as Fancy observed with a touch of hysterical laughter, in the same chair that had held her earlier callers. There seemed nothing left to do but seat herself.

For a moment the cool gray eyes locked with the fiery green ones. Finally the Earl spoke. "I collect you have had a busy day," said he in evident amusement.

"I fail to see that that is any concern of yours," returned Fancy tartly.

"*Au contraire,*" replied Morgane. "Castleford *is* my concern. We have been friends for a long time and I've no desire to see him make a gudgeon of himself."

Fancy felt her hackles rising. "I fail to see how making an offer of marriage to me makes the Marquis a gudgeon."

"So I was right. He did make you an offer."

Too late Fancy realized that she had swallowed the bait dangled so temptingly before her. "You tricked me!"

"If you would curb your temper, my dear, you would improve your character considerably," said the Earl with a cynical smile.

Fancy, vexed beyond measure, made a valiant effort to control herself. "Castleford's affairs are no concern of yours. Besides, he told me himself that you had given him carte blanche, relinquished the territory, so to speak."

The Earl's eyes kindled, but his tone was even. "I was relying on your known antipathy for male affection. But I did not suppose the fool would offer you marriage. At least, not until lately. I would, of course, wish to prevent him from taking such an ill-advised step."

"Of course!" cried Fancy hotly. Unable to contain her anger any longer, she rose and began to pace the floor. Her fingers itched to fling something at the Earl's urbanely smiling face, but she restrained herself. How that man could put her out of temper!

"Come, come," said the Earl, "did you accept him?"

"I did not!"

"Good, you have earned my approbation. You are more kindhearted than I supposed. Surely you have no aversion to being a marchioness."

Fancy stopped her pacing to glare down at him as he lazed in the chair. "You may make yourself easy on *that* head. I have an aversion to marrying a man for whom I have no strong feelings of affection," she declared hotly. "As I have imparted this information to you on several previous occasions I should think that it would come as no surprise to you."

"Perhaps you prefer to be York's favorite," suggested Morgane in even tones. "He would not ask

173

you to leave the stage. However, I feel that I should remind you, as I have already done, that my terms are better than York's. For whatever he promised you I am confident that in the long run you should do better with me."

Fancy could bear it no longer. Out of reason, cross, she stamped her foot on the floor. "You are insufferable," she screamed.

"Of course I am," interjected Morgane. "But is it necessary to inform the whole world of the fact?"

Fancy fought to control herself. She would not let this odious creature so wind her up that she would make a spectacle of herself before her household.

"The Duke of York's business with me is of no concern to you," she said between clenched teeth. "And I will thank you to keep your nose out of my business."

The Earl smiled. "In your present incensed condition I hesitate to disagree with you, but I find the whole affair of great concern to me."

Fancy's hands clenched into fists, but she managed to keep her voice low. "I fail to see how that can be so."

The Earl rose suddenly, causing her to step backward so precipitately that she would have fallen over a chair had he not reached out to steady her. At his touch Fancy found a strange weakness assailing her. She summoned a look of icy hauteur. "I have quite recovered my balance, thank you, milord."

For several long minutes the Earl did not remove his hands from her arm. His face was disturbingly close to hers. For a moment Fancy feared that he would kiss her again—feared and longed for what she feared.

Then, with a sharp laugh, the Earl released her. "Since the day I laid eyes on you in Bath," he said dryly, "you have been much on my mind."

Fancy drew herself up hotly. "I have told you more than once. I—am—not—for—sale!"

The Earl's handsome features took on a look of harsh determination. "And I have told you—I always get what I want. Always."

The Earl's eyes held hers for several seconds and then he bowed ironically. "No need to see me to the door, my dear. I know my way by now."

And then he was gone. Fancy stood for several more minutes and then, her legs suddenly unwilling to support her, sank into a chair and dropped her head into her hands. He was top-lofty, arrogant, odious, tyrannical—the most horrible, detestable man she had ever had the misfortune to know. She would never go willingly into his arms as he had said she would. Never. But oh, God, she thought, quivering with fright as the sudden knowledge struck her, she *wanted* to.

Chapter Eleven

The days passed quickly. Morning rehearsals, afternoon rehearsals, fitting of costumes, visits with the
dressmaker came and went. Fancy played her part
in *The Blind Boy*, reviewed her lines for *The Busy-
body* and *The Successful Husband*.

The crowds continued to riot. It seemed to Fancy
that nothing would be right again. Placards and
banners hung everywhere. Fruit, eggs, peas show-
ered upon the stage. Bow Street Runners, lent to
the managers, sat among the crowds armed with
bludgeons and from time to time charged and
overwhelmed some particular rioter before they
dragged him off to prison.

The pugilists, under the direction of Dutch Sam
and Mendoza, also attacked the rioters. But it was

like trying to hold back the ocean with a meager strip of sand. The swell of rioters rose and fell, pushing out around those intent on restraining them. And to Fancy's horrified eyes it seemed that for every rioter that was dragged away two more magically appeared to add to the general harassment.

Every evening Castleford and Morgane appeared in their box. Occasionally Castleford came back to the greenroom to congratulate her on her performance, but Morgane remained away. Fancy was quite grateful for this. She told herself so with considerable firmness. But still, every evening she crept to the wings to look out at the box that held the impeccably dressed, top-lofty Earl of Morgane. Sometimes she raked herself over for doing such an addlepated thing, but nevertheless she could not help it. She must know, before she set foot on that stage, that the dark Earl was there. And when inevitably he was, she felt a considerable sense of relief.

Even the jibes that Annie threw her way on every possible occasion now failed to set her back up. She could not, Fancy told herself, be bothered with such nit-picking. There were considerably more serious things to be considered.

She would not, of course, concede it to the Earl, but it was puzzling how he had managed to make such a deep impression on her heart. He was certainly, in spite of his friend's protestations, an ill-mannered man. Every time they spoke to each other they seemed to come instantly to dagger-drawing.

He was, of course, handsome in a dark saturnine way, his scar adding a certain sinister charm. And those cool gray eyes could kindle into passion. He dressed well, too, with the elegance and propriety that marked him as a Corinthian.

But many of the beaux who had sought her out in the greenroom at Bath had been personable, well-dressed, *and* well-mannered. And they had meant nothing to her.

Many, many times Fancy pursued this bewildering puzzle. Why should she form a partiality for this man and no other? But she never came to any resolve about it, except thinking wryly that perhaps it was her mama's blood acting up. For certainly Mama had been an unsuitable alliance for Papa.

When this thought first entered her mind, Fancy smiled. But then it occurred to her that what Papa had offered Mama was an honorable marriage. And that, most assuredly, was the furthest thing in the world from the Earl's dark head.

At home Fancy had given the strictest of instructions concerning Hercules. He was to be kept on a leash at all times, she ordered brusquely. And if he escaped again she would have the head of the culprit.

But one day toward the middle of November, Mr. Kemble sent the players home early. Fancy, stepping down from the hackney that she had hired because her coach was not due to arrive for several hours, paid the driver and trudged wearily toward the house. Even her knock seemed tired, she thought.

And then, as Henry opened the door, Hercules came bounding from across the room and past her. "Hercules!" Fancy commanded. But to no avail. The dog was already galloping down the walk toward the street. "Hercules! Come here."

It was no use. With a sigh Fancy turned and made after the dog. If she reached him before he assaulted the Earl's door, she could just drag him home.

She quickened her pace as she turned up the Earl's walk. And then, to her surprise, the door opened to admit the dog and closed again sharply. It all happened so swiftly that Fancy could do no more than gasp and stare. It was impossible to tell even who had opened the door.

She straightened her shoulders. She might as well go after the dog. At least she could leave the Earl's residence when she pleased. If she returned home, she could expect another visit from the overbearing Morgane.

She grasped the knocker firmly and knocked. To her surprise the door opened immediately and she found herself facing the Earl. She could not imagine what had possessed him to open his own door, but she took a deep breath. "I have come for my dog."

The Earl looked around him gravely. "Has your dog escaped again?"

"Of course he has." Fancy found herself put quite out of temper by such effrontery. "You just this minute let him in."

"I think it would be wiser for you to step inside. After all, we should not want our neighbors to involve us in some sort of scandal-broth."

Fuming, Fancy stepped inside and the Earl closed the door. "Shall we go into the drawing room?" asked the Earl pleasantly.

"Give me the dog and I shall go," said Fancy hotly.

"The dog is being cared for by Phelps. Have no fear on that score. Come, let us be comfortable while we talk. Take off your cloak and bonnet."

Fancy shook her head. "I just want my dog."

The Earl shrugged. "At least you shall see how Robert Adam designed my drawing room."

"I did not come to call or to discuss achitecture," said Fancy as calmly as possible. "I just want my dog."

"I'm afraid that is not possible at the moment." His hand came to rest on her elbow and she found herself guided inexorably toward the drawing room. That it was larger and grander than hers was her only impression of it. For the Earl guided her to a chair, waited until she seated herself, and then pulled one up beside her.

Fancy looked at him in bewilderment. "I do not

understand why you are making sport of me."

The Earl raised a quizzical eyebrow. "I thought I was behaving with great propriety."

"What do you want of me?" demanded Fancy in exasperation.

"I very much enjoy your company," said the Earl.

At this statement Fancy could only laugh sarcastically. "How is that possible? Unless you like always to be coming to cuffs?"

"No," said the Earl. "But, as I stated before, your beauty compensates me for your vile temper."

Fancy tried coolness. "I do not understand your purposes, milord, in detaining someone who wishes to be elsewhere."

The Earl smiled darkly. "I have conceived a great desire to hear Catalani sing."

"So?"

"Kemble having canceled her engagement at Covent Garden, she has engaged to sing at the Haymarket. I desire you to accompany me to hear her."

"Me?" Fancy stared in amazement. "You must think I have windmills in my head to imagine I'd do such a thing."

"I think you will," replied the Earl, his eyes sparkling.

Fancy shook her head violently. "You mistake me, milord. I would never, under any circumstances, accompany you."

"You have not yet heard my terms," said the Earl.

"Your *terms?*"

"Yes. You have a dog. A rather odious animal, but I collect you are fond of him."

"Of course I am fond of him." Fancy's green eyes sparkled in indignation.

The Earl nodded. "I thought as much. Now, that dog is presently in my possession. I shall return him to you as soon as we have heard Catalani."

Fancy stared. "You cannot be serious! You cannot steal my dog. I—I shall go to the authorities."

"And who will they believe?" asked the Earl with evident glee. "A brass-faced actress or a peer of the realm?"

"I am not brass-faced!" retorted Fancy automatically, but she realized with sinking heart that the Earl spoke the truth. No one would listen to a complaint against him. "This is infamous!" she cried.

"Indeed it is," agreed the Earl. "But I warned you that I will use any means that come to hand to attain my desires."

"You are despicable."

The Earl sighed. "My dear, you are wasting your time. You may call me all the epithets you care to, the case remains the same. The dog stays with me until you consent to accompany me to hear the Catalani."

"Never!" cried Fancy.

"I should not say that if I were you," replied the Earl reasonably. "At the present time I have no intentions on your honor. I simply desire your company."

As Fancy patently did not believe this, he continued in the same reasonable tone. "May I remind you as to what I said at our little tête-à-tête after the theater? I expect you will come to me willingly."

Fancy drew herself up stiffly. "You much mistake me, milord, if you think that will ever be the case."

The Earl continued to survey her from cool gray eyes. "I collect that it will take some time. But in this instance I shall be satisfied to have your company to the opera."

"You are a hardened rake-shame," cried Fancy in distress. "I cannot be seen with you."

"Might I remind you," he said evenly, "that you have already been seen with me? Half the world believes that we had a late tête-à-tête the other night. Besides, as I have repeatedly pointed out to you, an actress cannot expect to keep a good character. The nature of her calling precludes it."

Fancy was excessively nettled by the Earl's high-handed remarks and even more so by the cool amused way he regarded her distress.

"Yes," he said, as though reading her thoughts. "I know I am despicable, infamous, odious. All those pejoratives that you wish to apply to me fit the case. I am also obstinate. And the means having come into my hands for attaining my end, I do not scruple to use them."

For some moments Fancy seethed in silence. It was obvious that no amount of talking would persuade the Earl out of his designs. "Give me the dog, I will do it," she declared, a sudden thought coming to her.

"Oh, no, my sweet. *First* we go to the opera, *then* I return the dog. It is not that I mistrust you, but—" He let the word hang in the air.

Fancy fought to keep from coloring up, but was unsuccessful.

The Earl laughed. "I am ahead of you there. Once you had the dog I collect you would spit in my eye."

Aware that he was right, she nevertheless bristled up. "And how am I to know that you will keep *your* word? That you will return the dog?"

Morgane straightened and his eyes hardened. "I am the Earl of Morgane," he said harshly. "My word is always good."

From the expression on his face Fancy was sure that it was, but she could not refrain from pinching at him a little. "You must excuse me, milord," she said with exaggerated sweetness. "I have not often dealt with gentlemen of honor."

This hit failed to score and Morgane remained cool. "Regrettable, but somewhat predictable considering the nature of your profession."

Fancy knew he was baiting her, but she could

not help responding. "As I have been at pains to point out to you, milord, there are in *my* profession *women* of honor, though regrettably, but somewhat predictably, you have failed to make *their* acquaintance."

"A hit," said his lordship with a cheerful smile. "You are a most entertaining companion, Miss Harper, a definite remedy for ennui. For besides your beauty you also have a sharp wit."

Fancy received this compliment in silence. He needn't think that he could get around her with sweet words. "Will you please be so kind as to tell me what I must do to get back that miserable animal?"

"Certainly. The next evening that you are not treading the boards we shall go to the opera. When will that be?"

Fancy considered thoughtfully. "I have no part in *The Roman Father* which plays Monday next."

"Capital!" said the Earl. "Now, I shall expect you to be your usual beautiful self. I should prefer a gown of very dark green. Have you such?"

Fancy nodded. It was one of her favorites, but of course she did not say so.

"Good. And wear your hair simply, no ostrich plumes. And no jewels."

This last rather took Fancy by surprise, but, since she had no jewels but her stage ones, except a simple string of pearls that had been her mama's, it was certainly no hardship.

"Have you a cashmere edged in green?"

"Yes."

"Then bring it. And as to your behavior"—Fancy stiffened but the Earl continued mildly—"I shall expect you to make every effort to be pleasant." He raised a hand to silence her protest. "I know that will be difficult for you, but I expect you to make the effort. You are, after all, an actress. Think of it as a role. And I, too, will be charming. Such, I believe, as you have never seen me. Have you any questions?"

"And when will Hercules be returned?"

"I will myself lead him to your door the moment we return from the opera."

"I will do it," said Fancy. "But I still think you are odious."

"Quite within the bounds, I assure you. There is perhaps, however, something you have not considered."

"Oh?" said Fancy. "And pray, what might that be?"

"Such an evening may serve to dissuade York in his pursuit. He is still determined to pursue, is he not?"

Fancy nodded. "Yes, but it will do him no good."

"York is a stubborn man, more than reasonably fond of women. He will not concede until he sees another has won."

"But then I shall never be free of his attentions," exclaimed Fancy in dismay.

"Softly, my girl, softly. I am just explaining the matter to you. Once York believes that you have

186

become my inamorata, he will desist in his pursuits. He is, after all, a man of honor."

Even in her anger the twisted humor of this did not escape Fancy. "Are there no men of *honor*," she cried indignantly, "who do not try to rob women of theirs?"

The Earl raised a dark eyebrow. "The world is as it is. The wise, rather than protesting against it futilely, learn its ways."

"Perhaps," returned Fancy with some asperity, "I do not choose to be wise."

"A regrettable decision certainly," replied the Earl. "And one I shall seek judiciously to reverse."

Fancy could only glare at him. Still, she was forced to admit that, on the face of it, his advice was quite sensible. One could get nowhere by swimming against the current, as she had learned long ago. "I am already prospering," she said, striving for a calmness she was far from feeling. "And I am doing it *without* a protector."

The Earl smiled. "But not, I collect, without the help of a man. Now, now." He waved her into silence. "I am inclined to believe your story about not ever having seen Cavendish, but nevertheless, he was a man—and responsible for your present plump pocket. Was he not?"

Fancy could not avoid the truth of this statement. That was one of the most vexing things about the Earl. He could speak the truth and make it sound like something it was not. "I never met the Marquis of Cavendish," said Fancy evenly. "I believe he was some distant relative of Papa's, but I do not know just how. All I know is that he left me his house and the money to maintain it."

"Cavendish was a weird sort," commented the Earl. "Just the type to do something outrageous like that."

Fancy glared at him. "What is so outrageous about a man leaving some property to a distant relative?"

"Cavendish did not leave his property to 'a distant relative,'" said the Earl with a strange smile. "But to 'a beautiful redheaded actress.' One he knew would set the neighborhood all on end."

"Why should he do that?" asked Fancy, intrigued in spite of herself.

"Because he wanted to set their backs up."

"Are you telling me that the Marquis left me that property in order to get back at his neighbors?"

"Precisely," replied the Earl cheerfully. "And he succeeded, did he not?"

"I'm sure I don't know," replied Fancy. "I have been a good neighbor."

"Oh, indeed," replied his lordship with that lazy smile that so outraged her. "The gentlemen all tip their hats and bow, do they not?"

"Of course. They are most polite. And so am I. I am not the hurly-burly girl that you imagine me to be."

The Earl chuckled. "The ladies of the neighborhood do not see you as a hurly-burly girl either.

They see you as a beautiful incognita who may make a connection with one of their men."

Fancy sniffed disdainfully. "They can have their stupid men. I don't want them."

"But, my pet," explained the Earl, feigning not to notice Fancy's adverse reaction to his endearment, "*they* do not know that and therefore they view you with somewhat jaundiced eye."

Fancy shook her head defiantly. "If they choose to bother themselves about me, that is their concern, not mine."

"Certainly an admirable attitude. Very like my own," agreed Morgane. "But not one calculated to bring one many friends."

"You know very well," declared Fancy hotly, "that no *lady* in this neighborhood would ever be *my* friend no matter how circumspectly I conducted myself."

Morgane nodded. "Your understanding is quite good. You have brains as well as beauty."

Fancy stirred restlessly in the chair. "If you have no other orders to give me," she said with some sarcasm, "then may I go? I am excessively tired."

"Of course," said the Earl in his most solicitous tones. "The theater is too much for you."

Fancy felt the tears of frustration rising to her eyes. Would he never stop pinching at her? "I *love* the theater," she cried. "How many times must I tell you that?"

"Gently, gently, child," said the Earl, helping her to her feet. "I do not mistake your love for the stage. I merely think it love misplaced, better given to a man who could return it. Not to a bunch of rabble-rousing monkeys whose idea of fun is to throw orange peels and apple cores, who will never appreciate you."

Some strange emotion glimmered in the Earl's eyes as he spoke, but Fancy could not fathom it. She was very conscious that her hand still lay in his and that he was far too close to her for comfort.

She pulled her hand away. "I must go now," she muttered. "Henry is waiting for me."

Morgane's eyes met and held hers for a long moment. Then he smiled lazily. "Of course. An inestimable retainer, Henry."

With his hand on her elbow the Earl guided her to the front door. "Do not be concerned over Hercules," said he. "Actually he is quite happy here. Prefers my establishment to yours in point of fact. At least, that seems to be indicated by his efforts to enter it."

Fancy was feeling extremely exhausted. She and the Earl did not deal together at all well and being for long in his company made her excessively vexed.

He opened the door for her with an indolent smile. "Till Monday next, my pet."

With great effort Fancy kept her tongue between her teeth. The best thing to do was to take herself home, outside the Earl's purview. It was worse than useless to remonstrate with him.

So with an icy nod she made her way past him and down the steps. It seemed to take forever to traverse the short distance between the houses and every step she took seemed to Fancy to be subject to the ridicule of the arrogant man who stood in his open doorway watching her with that irritating lazy smile.

When finally she reached her own knocker, her barely suppressed fury caused her to knock much louder than she had intended. Henry opened the door, took one look at her face, and prudently refrained from comment.

"Hercules will remain at the Earl's until Monday next," she exclaimed. "I am excessively angry. Do not let anyone near me for at least an hour."

"Yes, Miss Fancy," Henry replied as she stamped up the great stairs.

Fancy entered her room, yanked savagely at the strings of her bonnet, threw it roughly in a chair, and cast herself between the deep green curtains onto the great bed.

He was arrogant, tyrannical, haughty, top-lofty, odious, the most despicable creature she had ever had the misfortune to know. Yet in that brief moment in which their eyes met she had wanted him to kiss her again, wanted it quite badly, in fact.

With a sob Fancy rolled over and buried her face in the pillow. And now she had promised to spend a whole evening in his company!

Chapter Twelve

Fancy hardly knew how she got through the inter-
vening days. She continued to rehearse and to play
her parts. And every night she could not refrain
from peeking out of the wings to see if the Earl
had arrived yet. Her heart beat in trepidation
when she thought of sitting in a similar box with
Morgane beside her.

When she considered such a thing, she was conscious of very mixed feelings. Some ridiculous
childish part of her insisted that it would be fun
to be escorted to the opera by the Earl. And he
had even promised to be charming! That, thought
Fancy, would certainly be unusual.

She was aware, too, that any woman who graced
the arm of the Earl of Morgane would be the object
of envy from other women. Though she had never

seen Morgane with a woman—he and Castleford were the only occupants of their box—Fancy had known without being told that women were attracted to the darkly handsome Earl. Probably all kinds of women—from young girls at their first come-outs to respectable married women—felt that strange power that emanated from the Earl. And if he really could be charming, how could any normal woman fail to succumb?

Of course, Fancy told herself when she reached this point in her deliberations, she was *not* any woman, and certainly not "normal" in the sense of dangling after a husband, or, at the least, a protector.

Take that young snip, Annie. She had certainly been going around with her nose in the air. Just last week a young Viscount, newly down from Harrow and not yet of age, had languished at Annie's feet. And the foolish girl had begun to chatter to her friends about leaving the stage and becoming a great lady. Fancy recognized the fact that a young man still under his father's control had little hope of choosing for himself unless that "choice" coincided with one already made by his zealous parent. The young Viscount might languish all he liked and gaze mournfully with great puppy eyes on the object of his affections. But such love was doomed to an early demise, being not vigorous enough to withstand the onslaught of an irate papa.

With a sigh Fancy saw the Earl enter his box. He was his usual impeccable self and her heart began to flutter at the sight of him. She was being ridiculous, she told herself, quite ridiculous. The Earl of Morgane meant nothing to her, nothing at all. That she did not succeed in convincing herself of this was clearly evident in the continuing flutter of her heart on every subsequent night.

And so the portentous evening arrived and Fancy stood before the cheval glass, radiant in the gown of deep green silk. Its rounded neck exposed a lovely white throat. It was caught high under her bosom and fell in graceful folds to her feet which were clad in matching kid slippers.

Ethel, who had insisted this once on helping her to dress, managed a smile. "You're a real beauty, you are," she said in admiration. "Your mama now, wouldn't she have been that pleased to see you grow into such a beauty."

Fancy could only nod, silently wishing that Mama was around to give her some much needed advice. For her heart was thumping quite dangerously and the high color on her cheeks was that of nature, not of the rouge pot.

She turned suddenly, unable to bear the sight of her own sparkling eyes. "Ethel, oh Ethel, I'm scared."

Ethel made a face. "Fancy Harper ain't afraid of nothing, not especially some high-flying lord."

Fancy gulped. "But all those people, Ethel, lords and ladies of the first stare of fashion."

"Listen, Miss Fancy, that Earl may be a hard

'un, but he knows his business with the ladies. He couldn't of made no better choice than that dark green. And I never did favor them stupid ostrich plumes, make a woman look like a ninny, they do. Yes, sir, you looks the very pink."

Fancy managed a little smile. "Thank you, Ethel."

"The two of you'll be the talk of the town," said Ethel with obvious satisfaction. "His dark looks is just the thing to set off your fair ones."

Fancy felt her heart lurch. He *was* extremely good-looking—the Earl of Morgane—the best-looking man she had ever seen. And there was about him that inexplicable thing that spoke of power, power over men—and over women. A shudder ran over Fancy.

"You'll be needing your shawl all right," observed Ethel. "There's a deal of shoulders a hanging out there."

Fancy flushed. "I mustn't forget my new kid gloves and my reticule, too." And she gathered up these items and prepared to descend the great staircase.

She had just reached the bottom when Henry opened the door to a brisk knock and the Earl entered, smiling urbanely. "I see that you are not a woman to keep a man waiting," he remarked. "A woman after my own heart."

Fancy scrutinized his face, but there was nothing in his eyes but pleasant warmth and his smile, too, reflected nothing but charm. She moistened her suddenly dry lips. "Thank you, milord. You look rather well yourself this evening."

She let her eyes wander over his muscular figure. His blue coat with gilt buttons fit his broad shoulders like a second skin. His drab-colored breeches clad a leg that any actor would give his eyeteeth to have. White silk stockings, black slippers, and chapeau completed the picture.

The Earl's eyes twinkled. "Indeed, as the great Beau once remarked, 'I am all elegance and propriety.' It is these two, hand in hand, that give a man distinction, he claims. And of course," he added mischievously, "the knack of tying a cravat properly."

Fancy's eyes went automatically to the stiff white cloth that encompassed his neck. "The mathematical," revealed his lordship. "And tied in under an hour. That must be some sort of record."

Fancy, who was accustomed to the lightning quick changes of a player's life, found a giggle bubbling in her throat. "You would soon lose your roles if you took that long in the theater."

The Earl laughed, a pleasant, open sound that quite startled Fancy. "Yes, I expect that thespians must be extremely quick in these matters." He reached for the fur-lined pelisse that Henry held and before she was aware of his intention he was putting it around her shoulders. As his fingers slid beneath her copper curls to lift them from under the cloak they touched the nape of her neck. An indescribable sense of weakness enveloped her, but, conscious of the presence of Henry, she managed to keep her face from reflecting her inner turmoil. Fancy Harper would never surrender to a man. And most assuredly not to the one who stood so securely before her.

"Shall we go?" he asked.

Fancy nodded and timidly put her hand upon the arm he offered. She was still slightly dazed. If this were an example of the Earl's charm she had best be careful. The Earl was a new man. Gone were the supercilious curl of his lip, the light of mockery in his eyes, the cynical set of his chin. These were replaced by a warm smile and laughing eyes.

Fancy felt rather inclined to give herself a good sharp pinch. This could not possibly be the Morgane she knew. With the greatest deference he assisted her into his coach, the warmth of his hand reaching hers through both pairs of gloves and causing a strange sensation in her heart.

"You are strangely quiet tonight," remarked the Earl, after they had driven for some moments in silence. "I hope that the nightly commotion at the theater has not begun to prey upon your nerves. I believe the proprietors will soon be forced to concede."

His tone was so considerate and concerned that Fancy looked at him in surprise, expecting to find some evidence of mockery in his dark face. But the shadows hid his scarred cheek and in the light of the coach lamps she could see only a pleasant, smiling man.

"Yes, I expect they will," she returned.

"The experience has been a difficult one for you."

Fancy nodded. "Yes. I have always loved the theater. As a little girl I pestered my mama for a part."

"And did she allow you upon the stage?"

Fancy shook her head. "No. Mama said it wasn't the thing for a nobleman's daughter. But then, when I was eight, she died. And Papa, too."

Fancy bit her lip to keep back the quick rush of tears. Lately she had been missing her mama a great deal.

"And you were left an orphan?"

Fancy swallowed hastily. "Yes, but Henry and Ethel were there. And they took care of me. And I went on the stage."

"And so filled up the empty space in your life." It was said so quietly that for a moment Fancy doubted her ears. He did seem to understand. How low his voice had been—and how strange.

"Yes," agreed Fancy. "I made the stage my life. And so—here I am."

For a moment the quiet was broken only by the sound of the coach moving over the pavement. "How do you suppose your mama would respond to your present way of life?" he asked quietly.

"She—" Fancy stopped suddenly, aware of something that she had never considered. It was quite likely that Mama would not at all approve of her being on the stage. "She—she wanted other things for me," faltered Fancy. "She didn't want me to be an actress. But, but, *she* was an actress. And she loved the stage. If she were alive now"—she found she had to swallow hard several times—"she would see how much I love it. And she would understand."

Surprisingly no objections to this issued from the man beside her. There was a moment's pause and then, in the gentlest of voices, he inquired, "Did your mama wish for you a life of celibacy, too?"

"No," said Fancy slowly. "It was not that we discussed it, but I am persuaded that Mama would have wished me to marry."

"A wise woman, your mama, very much concerned for your welfare."

"Yes," replied Fancy. "She loved me a great deal, I am sure." Fancy no longer felt the strangeness of the Earl's attitude. She had forgotten his arrogance and pride and was talking to him as though he were a friend.

"Have you never considered matrimony?" asked the Earl, still in that gentle tone.

"Not really," said Fancy. "For I've seen so many examples of marriage—and all bad. People who couldn't stand each other shackled together for life. Why, it's enough to frighten anyone."

"Indeed, it is," said the Earl soberly. "But I collect your mama and papa were happy."

"Oh, yes," agreed Fancy. "Very much so."

"Then perhaps," suggested the Earl, still in that

strangely gentle voice, "*you* ought to consider the possibility of finding such happiness."

"Perhaps I ought," agreed Fancy. "But happiness is not found in the marriage, but in the partner. And how can one be sure she has chosen wisely?"

"How indeed?" asked the Earl.

The coach now approached the King's Theatre in the Haymarket and slowed down. From outside could be heard the sounds of hooves, rumbling wheels, and shouting coachmen, each intent on gaining way for *his* master.

"Before we arrive at the theater I have a request to make of you."

Fancy was instantly on the alert. She may have let his gentle tone lull her into speaking honestly of her mama, but that did not mean that she had forgotten who he was! "What is it?"

The Earl chose to ignore the sharpness of the query and continued. "I have recently taken on approval a small set of emeralds. I should very much like to have you wear them this evening so I may observe their effect."

For a moment Fancy considered. As he had asked, she had worn no jewels. And out there in the lamplight were descending many lords and ladies, each of whom glittered with diamonds and decorations. With emeralds at her throat and wrist, she would feel more able to hold her own. With emeralds she realized suddenly, she could take on the role of lady. And then no one could touch her.

It occurred to her to wonder for whom the emeralds were destined; perhaps Morgane was giving up the pursuit of her and had settled on some other inamorata. However, that seemed unlikely, though perhaps he had an old one that he was keeping in hiding. Well, thought Fancy, that was certainly no concern of hers. None at all.

She gave him a small smile. "I will wear the emeralds, milord."

"Fine." From beside him on the seat he drew a velvet-covered box. "If you will turn your back to me, I will adjust the necklace."

Obediently Fancy turned. The jewels lay cold against her skin, but his fingers, as they touched the nape of her neck, were exceedingly warm. They seemed to linger there overlong and when, involuntarily, she made a small movement to escape them, he merely said, "Just a moment longer. The clasp is difficult in the darkness. There."

As his fingers left her neck she swung back around to face him. "Can you manage the earrings?" he asked.

"Of course." Quickly Fancy drew the wires through her ears. The earrings were long, she saw, long and narrow, and they sparkled in the lamplight. She had barely fastened them when the Earl was clasping something around her wrist. But there was little time to look.

The coach had halted and Morgane sprang out to help her down. For a moment she stood shivering on the pavement and then he was beside her, wrapping her more carefully in the cloak and guiding her toward the door.

The inside of the opera house was every bit as grand as the crowds entering it, but to Fancy it did not seem unusual. She was used to the grand insides of theaters. What was strange was to be on this side of the curtain, she thought. If she were at Covent Garden now, she would be in the dressing room, getting made up and costumed, her heart beating fast at the prospect of facing that howling, raging mob that served for an audience. Curiously Fancy looked down into the pit. Here dandies pranced back and forth with mincing steps, nodding to their acquaintances and ogling unknown ladies. There, others were busy cracking nuts or peeling oranges, cheerfully consigning the debris to the floor or just as cheerfully tossing it at a fellow swell.

With a great sigh of contentment Fancy leaned back in her seat. The whole world had not gone mad. It was only at Covent Garden that the crowd was vicious and angry. Here was the same spirit of camaraderie and fun that she had known at Bath.

"You sigh very deeply," observed the Earl as his hands moved to adjust the shawl which he had carried in for her.

Fancy smiled. "It is like coming home," she said. "This is the kind of audience I used to know. I had almost forgotten what it was like."

The Earl smiled, too. "I am glad you are enjoying the evening." His eyes lingered on her throat. "I must thank you for wearing the emeralds for me. Though they are so dimmed by your beauty that I doubt I can judge them adequately."

Fancy flushed at this compliment given with great sincerity and lowered her eyes. They fell upon the bracelet clasped around her wrist and an exclamation of surprise escaped her lips. A small set of emeralds? The stones were very large and very lustrous and they were surrounded by what could only be diamonds. "Milord!" Fancy faltered, her other hand flying to her throat where the equivalent of a king's ransom must be hanging.

"Yes?" The Earl's eyes were full of laughter, but it was warm laughter.

"A *small* set of emeralds!" protested Fancy. "I—I cannot wear these. They are too fine."

"Nothing is too fine for your beauty," replied the Earl solemnly. "And the jeweler from whom I had them will be most disappointed if you remove them now." He laid his gloved hand over hers as she strove unsuccessfully to undo the clasp of the bracelet. "You see, I promised him that they would be worn by the most beautiful woman in London—and I do not want to go back on my word."

His hand still clasped hers and Fancy tried unsuccessfully to keep down the flood of color that rose to her cheeks. "You—you flatter me."

Morgane shook his head. "You are wrong. Look across the way. See the box with the auburnhaired charmer?"

Fancy looked and nodded. The woman was indeed a beauty, dressed in off-white satin, her only adornment a pair of dangling ruby earrings. "She is very lovely," whispered Fancy in awe, seeing the many beaux congregated around her.

"That is Harriette Wilson, London's leading demi-rep," said the Earl. "And any of those bucks clustering at her sides like so many bees around a flower would give half his estate to change places with me."

Fancy colored up again. She could not be that beautiful. "You must be mistaken, milord," she faltered.

Morgane shook his head. "I think not. Intermission will prove me right. This box will be swamped by bucks of every age and description, endeavoring to get close to my goddess in green." And his eyes warmed in admiration of her.

Again Fancy felt that thrill go over her. Now it was crystal clear to her why the Earl could have any woman in London. "Milord," she stammered. "You embarrass me with such praise."

The Earl shrugged a nonchalant shoulder. "Over there, in the brown suit, the beau with the beaky nose, is Lord Petersham. He has been ogling you these ten minutes. To your right in the box with the blonde is Poodle Byng, so-called because of his curly locks. He, too, has been ogling."

"And there is Colonel Mackinnon," cried Fancy, quite forgetting herself.

The Earl eyed her sharply. "Have you met the Colonel?"

"Oh, no," replied Fancy, gazing around her in admiration and quite impervious to the steely look that had crept into his eyes. "I saw him in the park the day—" She stopped suddenly, unsure how to avoid mentioning his friend.

The steel left the Earl's eyes as quickly as it had come. "I collect that was when you went riding in Hyde Park with Castleford."

Fancy turned startled eyes toward him. "How did you know that?"

Morgane chuckled. "The whole *ton* knew before the day was out. All the bucks were abuzz to discover who was the new charmer. But I knew. There could only be one woman as beautiful as those descriptions said."

Fancy felt her color rising again. And when, in her confusion, she turned away to look out over the theater, she realized that she was being ogled by more than one pair of male eyes. In even greater confusion she turned back to the Earl. "Milord!"

Morgane's hand reached out to cover hers in a gesture that was strangely comforting. "Play your part," he whispered. "You are the most beautiful woman in England, wearing emeralds and diamonds to the value of £50,000. Now act it."

For one short moment Fancy panicked. Fifty thousand pounds! The thought frightened her terribly. But then the rest of his words registered.

Of course, she could not remove the jewels and run away. Fancy Harper never backed down from a part. Never. Her shoulders straightened, her head went up, and to the Earl's infinite amusement she stared down an upstart beau in a pink satin waistcoat with an élan that would have done credit to a duchess.

"You do the part well," he whispered admiringly.

Nevertheless Fancy was exceedingly glad to find the curtain going up. It was going to be a real treat to hear the Catalani.

As the slight dark figure moved onto the stage Fancy leaned forward for a better look and then sighed. Angelica Catalani had delicate black beauty. Jet eyes in a pale face were set off by masses of sable hair. No wonder all London lay at this woman's feet.

"Oh!" breathed Fancy. "She is beautiful."

The Earl nodded. "She is the toast of all London. A voice of great strength and sweetness."

And then the orchestra began to play and Fancy was caught up and enchanted by the lovely lilting tones. It really didn't matter a pin that she couldn't understand a word of the songs nor a thing about what was supposed to be happening. The music was sheer bliss. She shut her eyes and let it carry her where it pleased.

So enthralled was she by the glorious sounds that when the curtain fell for intermission she was suprised to hear the Earl speak.

"And now you have heard the Catalani. What do you think?"

"Oh," cried Fancy. "She sings as beautifully as she looks."

The Earl raised an eyebrow. "Her recitativo is somewhat inexpressive and her adagio a little cold."

Fancy stared at him in surprise. Was the Earl also a connoisseur of the opera? But before she could put this question to him he spoke again.

"There is time now for a promenade. Should you prefer that I depart for a while so as to leave more room for your admirers?" he asked gravely.

"Oh, no, please stay." Without thinking, Fancy grasped his arm. She felt the muscles tighten under her fingers and for a moment she feared that she had offended him, but when she met his eyes he was smiling pleasantly. "That is," she faltered, "I am much better at my roles if I have a good audience."

Morgane's smile deepened. "I also collect that your usual chaperone is not present."

Fancy was bewildered. "My—chaperone?"

The Earl nodded. "A large hairy one, I believe."

A giggle broke from Fancy's throat. "Wouldn't he look a little strange sitting here?"

Morgane chuckled. "He might even add a few howls to the chorus."

The picture this gave rise to made Fancy laugh aloud and so it was that she did not realize that anyone had entered the box until someone spoke from behind her. "Morgane, you rascal. How did you achieve such a thing?"

Castleford came forward and from behind him poured a veritable deluge of beaux. Of all shapes and sizes, they crowded to the front of the box, kissed her gloved hand, made a few pleasantries, and at a look from the Earl departed to make room for more.

When the curtain rose again, Fancy had no idea at all how many had besieged her with compliments. And in the eyes of each she had read admiration and desire—and upon some occasions, fear. This last puzzled her considerably until she realized that Morgane stood beside her, scowling at any poor devil who had the temerity to stay overlong.

As the last of the beaux left the box, the Earl settled again into his seat. "Thank you, milord," whispered Fancy, leaning close with a mischievous smile. "Though you are not large and shaggy, I believe you make an admirable chaperone."

Something strange flickered in Morgane's eyes, before a warm smile came to chase it away. "I am a jealous man," he remarked with a twinkle. "And the fact is well known."

It was not until she had turned back to the music that the full import of his words struck her. Then she saw the previous scene in a very different light. Morgane had stood by her side like—like she belonged to him, she admitted to herself. And all those beaux who had passed before her in homage obviously believed as much. Her hand stole unconsciously to her throat where the eyes of many men had lingered. Obviously, too, those men knew the value of the jewels. And they believed them to be the Earl's gift to her. The price, she thought, bitterly, of her surrender!

Not even Catalani's lovely voice could wipe out the rage that now invaded Fancy's breast. He had tricked her! The Earl had tricked her into wearing his jewels. And no one would believe that he had merely loaned them. This evening had compromised her even more than their supposed late supper.

How she hated the man, she thought angrily. It had all been a trick. Even his charm and kindness. A terrible trick to get what he wanted. He would use any means, he had said, any means to attain his ends. Fancy straightened her shoulders under the shawl. The Earl must learn a lesson, she thought firmly. He must be taught that he could *not* have everything he wanted.

This decision helped to assuage her anger, but she found that her rage was replaced by sorrow. Those had been precious moments, those moments of quiet talk. And to find that it was all part of his deception was very painful.

Still, Fancy was an actress and she played her role well. It was not until he had handed her into the coach and settled beside her that she rounded on him in anger. "You are quite the most despicable creature on the face of this earth," she cried.

The Earl seemed somewhat taken aback by this sudden tirade. "What, may I ask, has brought about this so sudden change?" he inquired dryly.

Fancy fumbled angrily at the jewels. "I have discovered the depths of your perfidy," she cried hotly. "You have tricked me."

"How so?" inquired the Earl.

"Those jewels," Fancy cried. "Your friends think you have bought me with them. But they are mistaken."

"Indeed, you wrong me," said the Earl evenly. "I knew you would not keep them. Indeed, I did not even offer them to you. And I did take them on approval. They could be yours, *if* you wanted them. But I thought you would not. Here. Let me undo them. I cannot return damaged merchandise."

The touch of his fingers on her neck seemed to increase her anger. "You knew what they would think," she cried. "You knew."

"I warned you before," said Morgane cheerfully, reaching for her wrist and unclasping the bracelet. "I always get what I want."

Fancy's fingers flew to her ears. "You will never get me," she panted as she removed the earrings and thrust them at him. "I cannot be bought."

Morgane received the earrings and returned them to the velvet-covered box. "I was not attempting to buy you," he observed calmly. "I am no fool. I was merely seeking to prevent anyone else from doing so. And I rather expect I have established myself reasonably well."

Fancy drew the cloak around her. "You may have succeeded in keeping the others away from me," she said. "And, since I should find their attentions troublesome anyway, I suppose I should thank you for it. At the moment, however, I find it a little difficult to generate any gratitude."

"I should think," said the Earl with that cynical smile and lazy drawl that she so detested, "that an actress such as yourself might at least try. A sweet kiss, for instance, might be appropriate."

Fancy glared at him in annoyance. "That is doing it up too brown," she declared hotly. "Why should I do such a thing?"

"Because you enjoyed the evening. You did, you know, until your brain began ticking away like some fanatic bluestocking. Come, be pleasant. It will not hurt."

Even as she shrank away from his arms, Fancy felt herself longing for them. But when he grabbed her and pulled her close, saying, "A little kiss cannot hurt your reputation now," she fought with all the strength she had.

Of course, all her strength was not enough and he crushed her to him, his mouth seeking hers. It was a different kiss, this one, not like the savage, punishing kiss he had stolen that day in his hall. This kiss began sweetly and gently, his lips teasing hers until, despite all her efforts to remain cold and lifeless, she felt her lips warm and open under his. For one endless moment that kiss suspended her in time. And then he was thrusting her from

211

him savagely. "You are no innocent," he declared angrily. "Not at all. You might as well let me keep you," he continued, his eyes gleaming wickedly in the darkness. "You already have the name. No one will ever believe in your innocence now."

"Because of you!" Fancy cried. "All because of you. I hate you!"

The Earl grabbed her by the shoulders and stared down into her eyes. "Love me, hate me," he said harshly. "It's all one to me. For I—I desire you. And I *will* have you."

For another long moment his eyes held hers captive. Fancy felt her limbs go weak. Part of her yearned to throw herself into his arms, to know to its fullest the passion that his kisses had roused in her.

And perhaps, had he approached her in some other fashion—but he had not, she told herself. He had not. And she could not be bought. Not even by a set of emeralds worth £50,000.

The rest of the journey was made in silence, Fancy staring into the darkness ahead of her and the Earl ignoring her presence. Finally they drew up to her house. Without a word Morgane helped her descend and escorted her to the door. He gave the knocker a quick rap.

"I shall return the dog immediately. And"—his mouth curled into the cynical grin—"I think you should know that I have not given up."

Fancy did not deign to reply to such nonsense,

but with a defiant toss of her curls swept into the house.

"The Earl will be returning Hercules," she told Henry as he shut the door. "Lock that dog up. And—do—not—let—him get out again!"

"Yes, Miss Fancy," replied the faithful Henry, watching her ascend the great stairs and smiling to himself in a strangely enigmatic way.

Chapter Thirteen

And so November wore into December. Fancy wrapped the fur pelisse ever more tightly as she hurried to her carriage during that first week in December. The rioters seemed indefatigable and she was sure that the Earl's prediction would prove correct. The managers would have to bow to the demands of the crowd—and soon, she hoped. For the strain was beginning to tell on her, since she refused to avoid the theater. She had come to London to learn everything she could about the stage. And so, even though the second run of *The School of Reform* was over and she had no part in *Young Rapid*, she went to watch Jones act it.

And there in his box, as handsome and as uppish as ever, sat the Earl of Morgane. He did not come to the greenroom when the evening was over.

Fancy, while she fought her disappointment, told herself that she was well rid of the highhanded Earl. But always his words rang in her ears, "I expect you to come willingly to my arms." And then Fancy would shiver.

Annie's young admirer was jerked home by his leading-strings and the girl became even more waspish than before, throwing out sly gibes at Fancy on any occasion she could manage. Fancy took this silently. There was little use in replying to such infantile behavior. There were other, graver things, much on her mind. And foremost among them was discovering the extent of her partiality for the Earl of Morgane.

And then it was Sunday again and Fancy faced another lonesome day at home. She rose early, in spite of leaving the theater late the previous night and before the sun was very high she had worked herself into as good a state of frustration as any ever evidenced by a tragic heroine.

Hercules, who had greeted her on her emergence from the bedroom, followed her down the great stairs and moved with her as she paced back and forth in the hall.

Once Fancy stopped to stare unseeing at one of the decorated panels. She had no recollection of how long she had been standing so, when she suddenly felt a cold nose thrust into her hand. Fancy smiled faintly. "Hercules, I can at least be sure of your love." But as she bent to scratch behind the shaggy ears, she remembered the Earl's voice say-

215

ing, "Do not be too surprised that he prefers the company of quality."

With an oath that would have astonished even Henry, she turned away and resumed her pacing. The Earl of Morgane was imperious, puffed-up, overbearing, and rude. And she wanted terribly to see his face close to her own, to have his strong arms enfold her again. "Fancy Harper," she said sternly. "You are becoming freakish. All about in your head, in fact. The Earl of Morgane is a hardened rake-shame, a libertine of the first water. He is wholly beneath the touch of one who wishes to keep her independence. Think no more about him."

It was this advice, considerably easier to give than to act upon, that she was still giving herself some hours later when the knocker sounded briskly.

Fancy, feeling her heart rise up in her throat and then fall again quite swiftly when the hearty tones of York informed her that the caller was not the one her heart yearned for, moved to the door of the drawing room to greet His Royal Highness.

"Miss Harper, my dear. You are looking quite lovely today."

"Thank you, sir," replied Fancy, shutting the door behind him. "I am feeling rather in the mopes. It is lonesome when I do not go to the theater."

The Duke shook his head. "I could never fathom how women fill up their days. Needlework. Ugh."

Fancy laughed at the expression on the Duke's open face. "Since I am an actress, I have little time

216

for needlework. I understand that ladies also enjoy cards and the races."

York brightened. "Quite true. And my duchess has her animals. Oatlands has become a menagerie. Not that I have anything against animals, mind you. But sometimes I think she's doing it up a little too brown. I mean, she must have close to a hundred dogs now."

"A hundred!" exclaimed Fancy.

"Yes." The Duke sighed. "And also there are monkeys, parrots, kangaroos, and ostriches."

Fancy suppressed a giggle. "That must make a large household for Your Highness to maintain."

The Duke waved a large hand airily. "I never have enough of the ready. There is no sense in thinking about that. But," he added with a plaintive sigh, "a man does wish on occasion to be able to sit in his own house without having to shoo away a dog."

Fancy managed to keep from smiling at this and waited expectantly.

York had not yet seated himself and now he came toward her and took her hands in his. "I hear that you attended the opera with Morgane. I suppose the emeralds are safely locked up. They must be worth a good deal."

"The emeralds are not mine," replied Fancy, withdrawing her hands from his grasp. "I only wore them as a favor to the Earl, who had them on approval."

"And you did not approve?" York shook his

head. "They were just the thing for you. More than I can afford, I'm sure."

Fancy bridled. "Your Royal Highness, pray listen carefully. The Earl of Morgane has the emeralds. I should never accept such a gift from him."

York's face brightened. "Then if you've rejected him, there is still a chance for me." And he took two strides towards her and clasped her in his arms. Fancy did not struggle. She did not fear His Royal Highness would go beyond a kiss. And a part of her was rather curious concerning how his kiss might compare to that of Morgane.

It was an adequate kiss, she decided moments later, but it had little effect on her. She was about to tell York something to that effect, though in a kindly way, when a deep voice sounded from the doorway. "My dear, I see that you have told His Royal Highness our good news and he is congratulating you."

York put Fancy from him with clumsy haste. "Your good news?"

The Earl nodded. "Yes, just last night Miss Harper consented to become the Countess of Morgane."

This piece of information was equally stunning to York and to Fancy. The Duke gathered his wits and made a quick bow. "I do indeed offer you my congratulations. This is—great news. I—I must go now. My brother expects me at Carlton House." With the air of a man who has been stunned by an unexpected blow he made his exit.

He was hardly through the door when Fancy, her eyes spitting fire at the Earl, moved to recall him. But Morgane was too quick for her. Before the words could leave her mouth, he had taken her in his arms and covered her lips with his own.

When finally he released her, the Duke's carriage was already making its way down the street. Fancy drew a deep breath. "You beast!" she cried. "How dare you!"

The Earl merely smiled, his eyes, under their drooping lids, regarding her with amusement. "I saw that the Duke was troubling you and so I thought to spare you his attentions."

"Was it necessary to tell him such a clanker?" demanded Fancy, still trying to regain her breath after that devastating kiss.

Morgane flicked an invisible speck of dust from his coat sleeve. "Perhaps not. But I was forced to think in a hurry. And that was the first thing that came to mind."

Fancy fought the urge to stamp her foot. "You have no right. What are you doing here anyway?"

The Earl looked around him, selected a chair, and settled himself in it comfortably. Only then did he speak. "My dear Miss Harper. I shall be glad to answer any question you care to put to me. But pray, do sit down and cease glaring at me like some irate fishwife."

With great effort Fancy restrained herself from letting loose a cloud of invective that would have aptly flowed from the lips of just such a person.

She forced herself to take several deep breaths. She would not give vent to her temper as the Earl expected her to. Carefully she selected a chair and settled into it, folding her hands gracefully in her lap.

Then she turned her eyes upon the Earl and inquired in the politest tones she could manage, "I should like to know why you have taken it upon yourself to march into my drawing room and tell the Duke of York the biggest Banbury tale ever."

"As I have more than once remarked," said the Earl, "I have an intense interest in your affairs. And, having observed York's carriage before your door, I came to your rescue."

"Rescue! Who says I needed rescue?"

A hint of steel appeared in the Earl's eyes. "You did not appear to be doing at all well in extricating yourself from the royal embrace and, since your chaperone seemed nowhere in evidence, I took it upon myself to come to your rescue. A dashed heroic thing to do, if I may so observe."

"Dashed stupid," reiterated the infuriated Fancy. "Telling York such a whopper. And who gave you the right to spy on me?"

Morgane sighed as though afflicted by a recalcitrant child. "Your choice of language betrays your lack of *ton*."

"I do not pretend to be a lady," cried Fancy. "But neither do I sneak around spying on people."

The scar on Morgane's cheek changed color, but his voice remained even. "May I remind you that living next door as we do, your visitors' carriages are plainly visible to me as I enter and leave my establishment? This being the case, as I exited to make a call on an old friend, I could hardly help observing York's carriage, arms and all, which incidentally was also fully observed by the rest of the neighborhood. Fearing for the safety of that virtue which you prize so highly, I sent my barouche back to the stable and sped to the rescue."

"I did not *need* rescuing."

"That, my dear, was impossible to judge from my position. True, you seemed to offer no resistance. On the other hand, however, you might have swooned and be lying lifeless in the villain's arms."

"Poppycock!" averred Fancy, putting down an urge to giggle at the picture Morgane's words presented to her. "I never swoon."

The Earl raised a nonchalant shoulder. "How was I to know that?" His eyes sparkled at her dangerously. "I collect that the business of rescuing maidens in distress may bring one few rewards. How fortunate that I live in an age where dragons no longer envelop such rescuers in their scaly coils, else I might have made my discovery too late to be of value to me."

Fancy fought hard, but the laughter could not be contained. It came bubbling out.

Morgane laughed, too, that open hearty laugh so unlike his usual sardonic chuckle.

"You are impossible!" cried Fancy when she could speak again.

The Earl continued to smile. "Perhaps, but I venture that since my advent into your life you have not suffered from ennui."

Fancy stared and then the laughter broke forth again. "I have never suffered from ennui," she replied. "I have never had time. But certainly your advent into my life has caused me considerable suffering."

"How so?" inquired Morgane with a lifted eyebrow. "I have offered you an establishment, jewels—an honest offer of keeping. I have driven from your door the droves of swells who lusted after your beauty. And I have just saved you from being another Mary Anne Clarke."

Fancy shook her head. "You put yourself rather high, milord. I have had admirers before, and I never needed anyone to protect me from them."

"Except Hercules."

"Except Hercules," she agreed.

"Still, if I concede to all that, I fail to see wherein I have caused you actual suffering." Morgane's eyes watched her shrewdly.

"You threatened me. You told me to leave the neighborhood."

"So I did," agreed the Earl, "but that hardly seems to constitute 'considerable suffering.'"

"You kissed me," Fancy cried. "Against my will. And generally made yourself obnoxious."

The Earl's lip curled cynically. "I kissed you," he conceded. "And against your will. Initially at least." With upraised hand he stopped Fancy's protest.

222

"But that I have been obnoxious—that I will not concede. Perhaps in the beginning. But not now. During our trip to the opera I believe I behaved myself with the utmost propriety."

Fancy remained silent, but her eyes were flashing scornfully.

"And surely whatever indiscretions I may have committed in my past pursuit of you may be forgiven by my actions today."

Fancy raised a quizzical eyebrow. "I am sorry, milord, but I fail to see how telling the Duke of York such a tremendous lie at all redeems you."

The Earl smiled strangely. "Suppose it were not a lie? Suppose I made you a real offer of marriage?"

For a moment the room seemed to whirl around Fancy, but she was no weakling given to fainting spasms. "I do not find your attempt at humor very amusing," she said finally.

The Earl straightened in his chair and his gray eyes met and held hers. It was like sinking in the ocean, Fancy thought, as she lost herself in the depths of those eyes. "I am a man of honor," he remarked with a wry chuckle. "And I am willing to stand behind my words to York. I will marry you."

For the second time Fancy's senses threatened to desert her. "You are flummering me," she said finally through dry lips.

Morgane shook his head. "Indeed, I am not. I shall cry the banns as soon as you say the word. And in a few weeks you will be a countess."

"You are mad," cried Fancy. "How can you think of such a thing?"

The Earl shrugged. "I have reached the age of two and thirty without losing my heart to a single eligible connection. Perhaps, as my friend Castleford says, it is time to settle down."

"But—but you don't love me!" cried a distraught Fancy.

For a moment the Earl's eyes clouded. "Love is an illusion for moon calves," he replied. "What is more to the point—I *want* you—and, as even I admit, barring the rising of your temper, you are an enjoyable companion."

"I am an actress," cried Fancy.

Morgane raised an eyebrow. "If you are now making reference to the whispers of the *ton*, you may be assured that they are irrelevant to me. I have no intention of wedding some whey-faced pimply chit in order to appease the whispers. And no one will insult you." His face darkened into a frown. "You can be sure of that."

"You are mad," repeated Fancy. "Even to consider such a thing. Castleford—"

"Castleford is my friend. He tried and failed. He will bear me no grudge. He is not that sort."

Fancy found that her hands were clenched in her lap. It seemed unbelievable that he should have offered her an honorable marriage. But he had!

Her heart pounded in her throat. If only he had said he loved her. Fancy moistened her dry lips. "I should be doing you a disservice," she said stiffly, "by marrying you in such case. Though you may not believe it, love is of vast importance in such things."

The Earl's mouth tightened. "I have offered you my name and my fortune. More I cannot do. Perhaps I have not made myself clear. Perhaps you would like to indicate the terms of your jointure. I have kept the emeralds. They will be yours. And any—"

"Stop! Oh, stop!" cried Fancy, jumping from her chair. "Do not speak to me of such vile things."

The Earl's mouth tightened further into a cruel thin line. "These 'vile things,' as you call them, are the realities of the world. Such chimeras as love will gain you nothing." He rose to his feet. "I believe I shall leave you to some contemplation. York will not expect any public announcement for a few days at least. Take time to consider. You are the first to be offered the chance to become the Countess of Morgane. Need I remind you that I am not exactly unsought after? Indeed, almost any anxious mama of unmarried maidens would consider herself blessed beyond measure by such an offer for her daughter."

"Then she would be foolish beyond measure," cried Fancy, driven quite to distraction by her desire to accept him on any terms and her efforts to fight that desire.

The Earl advanced toward her. "My offer still

stands. Should you change your mind, you know where to reach me." He bent low over her fingers and then he was gone.

In the warm room Fancy shivered. She had just turned away the man she loved. It was abundantly clear to her now that she loved him. And if he had once mentioned that emotion she would have flung herself into his arms and followed him anywhere on the face of this earth. But he had not and, as she stood there, two great tears rolled down her cheeks.

How could she marry him, loving him as she did, heart and soul, and knowing all the while that to him she was nothing but a toy?

Chapter Fourteen

And still the riots continued—the hisses, the cat-calls, the banners on the boxes, the placards in the hats, the O.P. war dances, the speakers dragged out by Bow Street Runners. There even appeared men with huge false noses who swaggered about the theater making carousal and others dressed like women who assailed those in the private boxes with coarse remarks.

And every night in the carriage with coachman, two grooms, and Henry to keep her safe, Fancy shrank from the hoarse cries and raucous laughter as rioters crowded people off the pavement and into the wet, dirty kennels. Through all of this Fancy could only sigh deeply. She was very disturbed by the change in her beloved theater, but she would not give it up. On that score she was quite determined.

And every night, no matter what the play, the Earl of Morgane appeared in his box. Sometimes Castleford was with him, but more often, especially after the first night of the play, the Earl sat alone in solitary splendor. One thing Fancy noticed was that no rioters ever came near Morgane's box, not to whistle or to harangue the crowd or to rail at him coarsely.

And Fancy could easily see why. Morgane's face, as he sat there seemingly oblivious to the clamor around him, was exceedingly stern. The cold gray eyes were fixed on the stage, the thin lips set firmly. Not by a single look did the Earl of Morgane condescend to notice the presence of the rioters. He lounged in his seat, as though in the utmost comfort, and stared fixedly at the stage.

Fancy could not understand the man, nor herself. Eight days had passed since he had offered for her, eight days in which it seemed that only the theater and her love for it kept her from losing what little sanity she had left. Certainly she knew that it was the height of madness even to consider marrying the Earl—a man who confessedly knew little and cared less about love. To marry such a man would just be asking for trouble.

And yet some perverse part of her kept insisting that perhaps it *would* work. And at least she could be with him. For Fancy was aware that every waking moment the thought of Morgane was with her.

Sometimes, most unexpectedly, she would hear the particular intonation of his deep voice resounding in her head. At other times his darkly handsome features would flash into her vision. And always there was within her the deep longing for the touch of his hand, the embrace of his arms.

"Bedlam," said Fancy to her reflection in the cheval glass as she tied her nightcap over her curls. "I shall be ready for Bedlam any day now if I keep on like this."

Then she turned from the mirror, blew out the candle, and crawled between the deep green hangings and under the featherquilt into the old bed. But she did not sleep. For a long time she lay muffled in the thick darkness, the curtain on the bed keeping out the least suggestion of light. Finally she sat up angrily and threw them back. She could at least watch the fire that flickered on the hearth.

And then, just as she was finally sinking into forgetfulness, there came the sounds of disturbance from below. There was a brisk knock on her door and Ethel hurried in, a lighted candle in her hand. "The Earl's below," she told Fancy. "He's come with his pistols."

"Pistols!" Fancy sat up quickly.

"There's rumors them rioters is planning to set Kemble's house afire." Ethel's usually dour face was even gloomier.

"But—but—" Fancy swung her feet down and

gasped as they hit the cold floor. "Why is the Earl *here?*"

Ethel set the candle down and groped for Fancy's slippers. "I ain't sure," she replied as she helped her mistress into them. "Henry's the one as let him in. But don't you go for to blame him for that. My Henry's a brave 'un, but the Earl—he's got them two pistols."

"Of course I don't blame Henry," said Fancy. "But I still don't understand why the Earl is *here.*"

Ethel, bringing Fancy's dressing gown and helping her into it, shrugged. "I'm sure *I* don't know. I ain't had much to do with quality and I ain't got no idea how their heads work."

Fancy tied the ribbons of her dressing gown and turned toward the door. "I guess I'll have to ask the Earl myself."

"Wait!"

Fancy turned in surprise and in a minute Ethel had whisked off the nightcap. "That Earl's got a sharp tongue," was her only comment. "No call to give him reason to use it."

As she made her way down the staircase, candle in hand, Fancy still could not understand Morgane's actions. But she did understand that her heart was pounding in her throat and the hand that held the candle was trembling.

As she reached the foot of the stairs she heard Morgane's voice coming from the drawing room. "Rouse the footmen, the grooms, the coachmen," he was saying. "And do it now."

Fancy drew herself up and entered the room to be met by a look of bewilderment from the obviously distraught Henry. "Milord, I must ask for an explanation of this strange conduct," she said firmly.

Morgane flashed her the merest of looks, but did not answer. "Do it now, Henry, we've no time to lose."

"Milord! Henry is not going to do anything until you have the courtesy to inform me as to the nature of this matter."

The Earl swung around to face her, his eyes glittering. "There's no time for courtesy now," he said harshly. "The mob has threatened to burn Kemble's house."

"Yes, I know that," said Fancy patiently. "But that does not explain why you are *here*."

"Because certain factions of the rioters have taken a dislike to a particular redheaded actress, a friend of Cooke's, and the rumor is that they may attempt to burn her house down around her ears."

Fancy felt a sudden wave of weakness hit her. "You mean—my house?"

The Earl nodded. "Now, Henry, hurry."

Henry waited for no further word from his mistress but moved quickly off.

"But why should anyone want to burn *my* house?" asked Fancy.

The Earl shrugged. "No one can find rhyme or reason in the actions of a mob. That is why they are so much to be feared."

231

As Fancy stood shivering, uncertain what to do or say, Ethel bustled in with some firewood and built up the fire that smoldered on the hearth. "It's a wicked cold night," she remarked to no one in particular. "Decent folk ought to be snug in their beds."

The Earl smiled sardonically. "Too bad the rioters are not of that sentiment."

Ethel soon had the fire blazing high; its cheerful warmth, combined with the glow of the addtiional candles that she lit, gave the room a more comfortable look.

"Here, now, Miss Fancy," said Ethel, taking a firm hold on her mistress's elbow and guiding her to a chair near the fire. "Do sit down here and get warm and I'll make a nice pot of tea."

She pulled another chair near the fire and addressed the Earl. "You might as well be taking the load offen your feet, too, your lordship. God knows, if a mob be coming here, we'll hear 'em soon enough."

"Thank you, my good woman. You have a head on your shoulders."

Ethel's only reply to this was a slight sniff of disparagement, but her eyes gleamed brightly as she hurried from the room and she was heard to remark to the frightened kitchen maids as she hustled in her task of making tea that the Earl weren't no common kind of lord. Not at all.

Fancy, still half asleep and frightened by the appalling vision of a riotous mob armed with torches, stared unseeing into the flames, her arms wrapped around herself and still shivering.

She was aroused from this terrifying vision by the touch of a warm hand on her cheek as the Earl adjusted a shawl around her shoulders. "Here," he said in that strangely gentle voice he had used in his coach on the way to the opera. "You are shivering."

"Thank you," Fancy murmured, pulling the shawl tighter around her. It was not the chill of the drawing room that made her shiver so, but the fear, fear of the beast that a mob could become. Such a beast could destroy everything she had.

Her shoulders trembled at the thought. And then two strong hands rested there. "Come, girl, where's your spirit? We'll keep them off. That's why I sent Henry to rouse your men."

Fancy, looking up into a pair of warm gray eyes, longed desperately to throw herself into his arms. There, she saw with sudden insight, she would feel safe—only there.

But she forced herself to sit quietly, forced herself to tear her eyes away from his before he could read her secret there. "Thank you, milord," she said. "It is only that—the audience, you see, has always been my friend. And now—" Another tremor sped through her body.

"You are freezing," said the Earl calmly, his hands moving down to pull her erect. Then, before she knew what had happened, his arms had closed around her and she had the feeling of security she

233

had so longed for. There in his arms all thoughts of mobs and fires vanished. Gradually she grew warmer and the trembling stopped.

And then Fancy grew aware that the arms around her had tightened and the heart under her ear was thudding heavily. If he should kiss her again—but then common sense came to her rescue. She could not marry him; she knew it. And it was dangerous to be so near him. Dangerous for them both, though he could not know it. Still, she could not bring herself to pull away. This was probably the last time she would feel his arms around her.

A sudden bustle was heard in the doorway and Ethel said, quite as calmly as though the whole room separated the two of them, "Here now, I've fixed you a nice pot of tea and here's some of them macaroons that chef man made."

The Earl removed his arms slowly, except for the hand that remained on her elbow to steady her. His face, as Fancy hazarded a quick glance at it, showed not the least embarrassment at being found in such a compromising position by a servant. "Thank you—"

"Ethel's my name," said that worthy, with a glance at Fancy that spoke volumes.

"Thank you, Ethel," said the Earl, seemingly oblivious to the exchange between the women. "We will now await the mob in comfort."

Ethel nodded. "Ain't no point in worrying about trouble you ain't got yet, I always says. Now, Miss Fancy, you drink up your tea. That'll keep you

234

good and warm." And with a sly smile, Ethel departed.

Fancy settled again into her chair. She wanted very much to steal a look at the Earl's handsome face, but her courage failed her. If he ever suspected how much he affected her, he would probably use that power without compunction. And, much as one part of her longed to surrender to him, her pride would not permit such a thing. Such a surrender would only make him more arrogant and top-lofty than ever. And she would never consent to becoming such an abject creature.

The Earl poured the tea and offered her a cup. "Thank you," murmured Fancy, keeping her eyes averted. She sipped the tea slowly, wishing that there was some way she could teach a man to love.

The minutes moved slowly and all was quiet. From time to time the Earl left the drawing room to check with Henry for the latest reports from the men he had posted down the street.

"You are very quiet tonight," he remarked on his return from one of these trips.

"I—I have little to say," replied Fancy.

The Earl offered her the plate of macaroons, but she shook her head. "I am not hungry."

"Have you been eating properly?" asked Morgane suddenly. "You are looking a little hagged."

For some reason this roused Fancy when nothing else had. "I'll thank you to remember," she said tartly, "that in the normal course of events I am not accustomed to being rousted from my bed in the

235

middle of the night to await the advent of a mob."

Morgane nodded. "This has been a trying time for you, facing those hostile crowds night after night. It's a strain on anyone, and especially on a woman."

Fancy found herself bristling up again. "I'll have you know I'm strong as a horse," she declared hotly. "And I'm holding up just as well as any of the men."

"Of course you are," the Earl agreed in such a placating tone that Fancy glanced at him in surprise. "I am only saying that the whole business has put you under considerable tension."

"Yes, it has." Fancy found this gentle-voiced Earl even more frightening than the arrogant, supercilious one. This was the one who had tricked her into wearing the emeralds. Just because he sounded kind and friendly was no reason to believe him so. As he himself had admitted, he would use any means, any means at all, to achieve his ends.

Another long silence ensued in which Fancy sat staring at the fire and the Earl seemed lost in his thoughts. Then he raised his head and surveyed the room through half-closed eyes. "Yes, an admirable room," he remarked. "Robert Adam had the knack for creating a room of beauty."

Fancy nodded. "The other rooms are equally well done. My bedroom, for instance, has one end of an oval shape that I understand was one of Adam's innovations. And, if I am correct, I believe that Angelica Kauffman did the small medallions in that ceiling."

The Earl's look of surprise turned to one of interest. "And what do you think of Adam's mingling of Roman and Pompeian motifs?" he asked.

"I believe that it works quite well," replied Fancy. And the next hours were spent in a spirited, but friendly, discussion of various aspects of Robert Adam's work.

The rising sun peeping through the drawing-room curtains caused Fancy to exclaim in surprise. "We have sat up the whole night!"

"So we have," replied the Earl nonchalantly. "And so I expect that the danger of violence from a mob being no longer an object for concern, I should make my way homeward before the neighbors—"

Suspicion entered Fancy's mind with the ease of a practiced snake in Eden. "The neighbors! What will they think?"

Morgane shrugged. "They will think what they have been thinking for some time. We have already become an *on-dit*. This will only serve to confirm them in their beliefs."

Fancy felt the irrational longing for his arms rising to choke her. And then pride came to her aid. He had said she would come willingly to his arms, but she would not surrender like that, especially now. She summoned her anger. "In the light of day I am not at all sure that the mob *ever* contemplated firing my house," she said stiffly.

The Earl's expression did not change, not by so much as the flick of an eyelash did he betray his anger, yet somehow Fancy was aware of it even before he spoke. "I realize that my word has little value to you," he replied calmly. "But even I would not wish to frighten you with the idea of a mob in order to drive you into my arms. I wish your surrender to be a willing one. And I am a patient man."

His eyes probed her, and Fancy, fearing to betray herself, looked away. "Well, you must admit that you warned me you would use any means. And—and I have seen you in action."

The Earl nodded and prepared to leave. As he bent over her hand Fancy swallowed quickly. "I— I do want to thank you. After all," she stammered on, "you did sit up all night. And—and you didn't— that is—"

The Earl gave her a frosty glance. "I suppose you are referring to the fact that earlier this evening— or morning rather—I held you in my arms and did not attempt to make any advances to you."

Fancy, coloring to her eyebrows, could only nod.

"That was obviously a deplorable neglect of opportunity," he commented dryly. "Not at all what one would expect of a man of my blackened character."

"Oh!" Fancy could find no adequate words with which to reply. "You are impossible!"

The Earl smiled cynically. "You are very beauti-

238

ful when you are angry," he said with amusement. "Perhaps most beautiful of all. But then, that may be because I most often see you in that condition."

He released her hand and moved to the table to collect his pistols. "I think it safe to send your people to bed now," he said briskly. "No mob is going to fire a house in broad daylight."

Fancy rose to her feet. "Thank you," she repeated, compelled by some demon to raise her eyes to his. What she saw there was raw desire, desire so strong that it quite took her breath away. And then the Earl's eyes grew veiled.

"Just to keep things clear between us," he drawled, in his most affected tones, "I believe I should remind you that our houses are wall-to-wall. Even if I had no other interest in you whatsoever, it would behoove me to keep your house from being put to the torch, since mine would be quite likely to go with it. And now—" His eyes sweeping over her cynically recalled to her the fact that she was still in her nightdress and dressing gown. "Now I suggest you return those pretty curls to your nightcap and get some sleep. I prefer that my women be fresh and clear-eyed."

And with a low chuckle the Earl departed, a pistol in each hand, and left a bemused Fancy staring into space. It was thus that Ethel found her some time later and took her up the stairs to bed. But even then, with the curtains drawn tight to keep out the rising sun, sleep was a long time coming to

Fancy Harper. Each word, each expression, must be relived, not once but many times. But always she came back to the same bitter realization. She could not marry a man who did not know how to love.

Chapter Fifteen

‖‖

The cold December days passed slowly for Fancy; there was always in the back of her mind that intense yearning for the sight of Morgane. And then, on December 14, Kemble assembled the players to announce that the rioting was over. The proprietors would capitulate to the demands of the crowd—reduce the prices and remove the extra boxes that had helped to cause so much furor.

As though touched by some magic wand, the audience became its old self and the rapport between player and crowd was reestablished. At first it seemed funny to Fancy that her lines could now be heard, but soon she began to forget the tensions of the past days.

But she could not forget the Earl of Morgane. Of course, she never looked at the audience while she was playing, but, when she was not on stage, it was her habitual practice to stand in the wings watching the performance. From this vantage point she also had a good view of the boxes, including the one that held the Earl of Morgane. But now he changed his habits and appeared in his box only when a new play was beginning its run. Some demon in Fancy's heart tormented her with conjectures as to the cause of the Earl's change of habit. Could it be at all possible that he had occupied that box night after night in order to insure *her* safety?

When she considered the soft-spoken, gentle man who had been her companion to the opera, it seemed entirely possible. But when she considered the disdainful, lofty man who had sworn he always got what he wanted, it seemed highly unlikely. And yet, he had been there every night when danger threatened her. And now that the danger was gone he was not there. Finally Fancy told herself angrily that if he *had* been there to protect her it was only because he regarded her as a piece of property that would some day be his. And she would never consent to being regarded in such a light.

So more days passed and Fancy, regarding her face in the cheval glass, frowned angrily. She was getting definitely hagged. Even her gowns were beginning to hang on her.

"How long are you going on like this?" demanded Ethel brusquely.

Fancy flushed. "Like what?"

Ethel shook her head. "Ain't no use you trying to bamboozle me. I seen the way you look at him."

"Ethel, I don't know what you're talking about."

"I'm talking 'bout the Earl of Morgane, that's what I'm talking 'bout. And you eating your heart out for him."

"Ethel! I'm not. I couldn't care less—"

Ethel shook her head. "You listen to me, Miss Fancy Harper. You ain't fooling me one little bit. I guess I know what love's about as well as the next one."

"I'm not—"

"Oh, yes, you are. Always mooning around here, heaving them big sighs and looking like some actress in a Cheltenham tragedy."

"Oh, Ethel!" Suddenly Fancy found the words pouring out. "He offered to marry me, but it was a mistake, a spur of the moment thing to convince York."

Ethel interrupted this explanation with a snort. "That there Earl never did nothing on the spur of the moment. He's a cool one, he is. And if he offered you marriage, it's Carlton House to a china orange, that's exactly what he *meant* to do."

"But Ethel, why?"

Ethel shook her head. "You surely ain't got much woman sense. He wants you, that Earl does. He wants you bad."

"But marriage?"

Ethel shrugged. "That Earl ain't no ordinary

243

lord, he ain't. You can be certain sure he knows *exactly* what he's doing."

"Oh, Ethel," wailed Fancy. "What shall I do? He doesn't love me."

"He wants you," replied Ethel with quiet common sense. "Many a marriage—and good 'uns, too —been built on that."

"But he doesn't know how to love. He doesn't even value love."

Ethel smiled dourly. "Many a man's been in love afore he knew it. And I wouldn't be all so sure about that Earl. Happen he might know a thing or two about love that *you* don't."

Fancy flushed again. "Ethel, don't make fun of me. I need help."

"What you need," said Ethel firmly, "is the Earl of Morgane. And now I got to see to it that that Frenchman in the kitchen wrestles up something decent for dinner. Some sound English food as a person can recognize when he puts it in his jaws." And Ethel marched out, leaving Fancy no closer to a solution than before.

"I do love him," she told herself. "Though I can't go tell him so. But I do need to see him."

At that precise moment the door was pushed open by a great shaggy head and Hercules advanced cautiously into the room. He had not been the particular favorite of his mistress for some time now and so he was agreeably surprised that upon seeing him Fancy uttered a joyous exclamation,

244

dropped to her knees, and threw her arms around him. Hercules, however, was not one to hold grudges, and he returned this embrace with a series of enthusiastic licks on whatever part of Fancy's face was available to him.

"Oh, Hercules, you wonderful dog. Come, you're going for a run."

Halfway to the door Fancy stopped and returned to the mirror to scrutinize her face and run a brush through her curls. Then she hurried out again, Hercules close on her heels.

It was a matter of moments to dispatch each servant found near the front door on some fictitious errand and then Miss Fancy Harper quietly opened that door for a great shaggy dog who eagerly slipped out. Smiling happily, then, she retired to her sitting room to await results.

If only Morgane wasn't gone out, she thought with trepidation. But it was still early and the Earl seldom made early calls. He would be home; he *must* be home.

As the minutes passed she took to pacing round and round the circular carpet, clenching and unclenching her hands. And then, finally, when she was about to give up all hope, came the longed-for knock on the door. It was not *his* knock; she knew that instantly.

And then Henry was at the sitting-room door. "It's Hercules, Miss Fancy. He's gotten out again." Henry shook his head. "I don't see how it happened. But the Earl sent his footman to say you've got to come after him. He don't feel like bringing him home today."

Henry's frown indicated that he expected some evidence of temper from Fancy, but she had no energy for counterfeiting anger. "All right, Henry. Where is his leash? I'll go get him."

Henry departed, to return speedily with the leash and a look of dawning comprehension. As he helped Fancy on with her fur-lined pelisse and handed her the leash, he whispered softly, "Good luck, m'girl."

Then Fancy was outside, pulling the cloak around her, hurrying down the wet steps and across the walk up to the Earl's door. For just a moment she stood trembling at the audacity of her actions and then she gave the knocker a brisk rap.

The door opened almost immediately to disclose the Earl of Morgane. Fancy's heart skipped a beat as her eyes met his.

"Come in," said the Earl formally. "I do not know why you cannot keep that abominable creature under control." He took her cloak and laid it aside. "He came bounding into my library and hurled himself into my lap to the absolute devastation of my inexpressables." His lip curled derisively. "It would save us both a good deal of trouble if you would accept my offer. The dog would obviously be happier, and I shouldn't have to fear being assaulted by that great furry beast every time my door is opened."

Fancy's heart still pounded in her throat. There he stood, the man she loved. And all he could speak of was clothes and dogs!

Suddenly the whole thing was too much for her. The tears rose unbidden to her eyes and poured down her cheeks while great sobs shook her body. She had been an utter fool to want to see him. Nothing would ever work between them.

Blinded by her tears, she turned back toward the door and ran into a broad chest. As the Earl pulled her to him she fought frantically. "Let me go," she sobbed. "You—you are the fool. Not to know love."

The arms around her tightened more forcibly and Fancy, giving up to the misery that overpowered her, stopped fighting and sobbed miserably against a warm waistcoat.

It was some time before she became conscious that one of his hands was patting her back in a comforting motion, almost as one would pat a baby. And she grew aware that in Morgane's arms she felt warm and secure, not at all menaced.

Suddenly she recalled the expression on Ethel's face as she commented that the Earl might know some things about love that Fancy didn't. With those warm arms around her things began to fall into place. Perhaps he *did* love her. After all, that girl in Germany had hurt him badly. Perhaps he was afraid to speak of love. And they had been always at cuffs—an unlikely situation for such disclosures.

247

Snug in the circle of those arms, Fancy made a decision. Love was worth risking for. It had to be.

Then, before she could frighten herself about the future, she spoke. "Morgane, I have come to accept your offer."

The Earl put her from him so swiftly that she almost fell. "My offer!"

Fancy nodded. "Yes, I will marry you."

The Earl seemed stunned. "Are you mad?"

Fancy shook her head. "I think not. What's the matter, milord, have you second thoughts about having an actress for a wife? Or wasn't your offer genuine?"

"Of course it was genuine!" The Earl's eyes flashed. He moved away from Fancy suddenly and took several turns around the room.

When he stopped in front of her again, he had regained his composure. "I am honored at your acceptance," he said gravely. "I shall have the banns called. But why, why the change of heart?"

It was now or never, Fancy thought as she brought her eyes to meet his. "I discovered something," she said. "Something important."

"The value of my estate perhaps or a sudden taste for emeralds."

The tears brimmed again in Fancy's eyes. What if she had made a mistake? What if he really were only cold and hard? But she forced herself to continue. "I'm afraid those things are beyond my

248

control," she said, fighting to keep the tears back. "Actually, I should prefer you *not* to have them. But the simple fact is this: I discovered that I love you."

For long moments the Earl stood silent, and Fancy, hoping frantically for some sign in his face, could see nothing there. Her heart sank, but she would not give up, not until she was sure.

"I know that you believe love is an illusion," she went on. "But it is not. It is the most important reality. And I warn you—" Her head went up and she took a step toward him. "I warn you. If you marry me, I intend to teach you to love."

For one silent moment their eyes met and then Fancy threw herself into his arms. As his mouth sought hers, she was praying. Dear God, she must be right. He must love her.

The kiss was warm and tender, passionate in a way Fancy had never before experienced. And when the Earl released her lips it was only to fold her close against his chest and whisper hoarsely into her hair, "That will not be necessary. I have already learned to love you."

Fancy looked up into his eyes, eyes suddenly gone warm and loving. "I hoped," she whispered, "but I could not be sure."

"I believe I loved you in Bath," Morgane explained. "But a woman once betrayed me and I vowed vengeance on their kind. And when you resisted me—"

"We did not get off to the best of beginnings," agreed Fancy. "But that doesn't signify now." She sighed in contentment. "I'm so glad I let Hercules out."

"You! Let him out?"

Fancy nodded, laughter bubbling in her throat. "But what I don't understand is why he always comes here."

The haughty Earl of Morgane took on a strangely sheepish look. "You! You arranged it!" Fancy cried. "But how?"

The Earl smiled, and taking her hand in his, led her to a door which he opened. There, in a small sitting room, reclined Hercules, a great bone still plentifully supplied with meat between his paws.

Fancy burst into laughter. "You fed him!"

The Earl chuckled. "The first time he came was an accident, but I knew he was yours and I made sure he would return."

"But you warned me away—out of the neighborhood." Fancy was suddenly grave.

Morgane's arm tightened around her waist. "I knew my feelings for you were different and I had resolved not to love again."

"And I had resolved *never* to love," said Fancy with a smile. "But love was too great for both of us."

And there, in the doorway of a little sitting room, Fancy Harper put her arms around the neck of the man she loved and raised her lips for his kiss. And the great dog continued to chew on his bone and wag his tail appreciatively. Humankind behaved strangely sometimes, Hercules thought, but now that these two had finally gotten together, things were definitely looking up.

Love—the way you want it!

Candlelight Romances

Dell Bestsellers

☐ **TO LOVE AGAIN** by Danielle Steel $2.50 (18631-5)
☐ **SECOND GENERATION** by Howard Fast $2.75 (17892-4)
☐ **EVERGREEN** by Belva Plain $2.75 (13294-0)
☐ **AMERICAN CAESAR** by William Manchester . . . $3.50 (10413-0)
☐ **THERE SHOULD HAVE BEEN CASTLES**
  by Herman Raucher $2.75 (18500-9)
☐ **THE FAR ARENA** by Richard Ben Sapir $2.75 (12671-1)
☐ **THE SAVIOR** by Marvin Werlin and Mark Werlin . $2.75 (17748-0)
☐ **SUMMER'S END** by Danielle Steel $2.50 (18418-5)
☐ **SHARKY'S MACHINE** by William Diehl $2.50 (18292-1)
☐ **DOWNRIVER** by Peter Collier $2.75 (11830-1)
☐ **CRY FOR THE STRANGERS** by John Saul $2.50 (11869-7)
☐ **BITTER EDEN** by Sharon Salvato $2.75 (10771-7)
☐ **WILD TIMES** by Brian Garfield $2.50 (19457-1)
☐ **1407 BROADWAY** by Joel Gross $2.50 (12819-6)
☐ **A SPARROW FALLS** by Wilbur Smith $2.75 (17707-3)
☐ **FOR LOVE AND HONOR** by Antonia Van-Loon . . $2.50 (12574-X)
☐ **COLD IS THE SEA** by Edward L. Beach $2.50 (11045-9)
☐ **TROCADERO** by Leslie Waller $2.50 (18613-7)
☐ **THE BURNING LAND** by Emma Drummond $2.50 (10274-X)
☐ **HOUSE OF GOD** by Samuel Shem, M.D. $2.50 (13371-8)
☐ **SMALL TOWN** by Sloan Wilson $2.50 (17474-0)

At your local bookstore or use this handy coupon for ordering:

SHARON SALVATO
co-author of *The Black Swan*

Bitter Eden

**He taught her what
it means to live
She taught him what it means to love**

Peter Berean rode across the raging
landscape of a countryside in flames.
Callie Dawson, scorched by shame, no
longer believed in love—until she met
Peter's strong, tender gaze. From that
moment they were bound by an unforget-
table promise stronger than his stormy
passions and wilder than her desperate
dreams. Together they would taste the
rich, forbidden fruit of a *Bitter Eden.*

A Dell Book $2.75   (10771-7)

At your local bookstore or use this handy coupon for ordering: